***Birds Are Liars* is like a book of** murmurations. Startling sentences soar and skitter across its pages in intricate patterns in the most mesmerising way. These stories of desire and loss, memory and uncertainty are often unsettling, always beautiful and surprising. Bernadette McBride has listened to the birds.

—Jeff Young, winner of the 2025 TLS Ackerley Prize, author of *Ghost Town* and *Wild Twin* (Little Toller Books)

**Bernadette McBride's stories are a tonic** for troubled times. Beautifully written, this debut collection shows us that if we could only understand the natural world—and ourselves—more fully, it might just save us from catastrophe. Superb.

—Ian Critchley, winner of the Hammond House International Literary Prize and the HISSAC Short Story Prize, author of *Removals* (Nightjar Press)

**Bernadette McBride is not afraid** to take risks, as this original and affective collection of short eco-fiction demonstrates. Lyrical—poetic even—and often formally surprising, McBride's fiction has the uncanny ability to not only connect with and move the reader, but to get right under their skin.

—Paula McGrath, author of *Generation* and *A History of Running Away* (John Murray Press)

**Evoking the texture of subjective** experience in the age of extinction, microplastics, and data centres—a world replete with energy and catastrophe, information and death—is no mean feat. McBride achieves it brilliantly in these evocative, formally daring short stories. Shot through with melancholy and wonder, *Birds Are Liars* reads like a visionary dispatch from a future so close we might as well be living it, with uncanny echoes of present events: "Warnings spread across Europe." But if McBride is clear-eyed about the damage wrought in the name of human progress—which may be coming back to haunt us—she is equally attuned to the indestructible capacity for tenderness and hope: "a bright light pierced the darkness like a fire in the air."

—Patrick Langley, author of *Arkady* and *The Variations* (Fitzcarraldo)

**Bernadette McBride's stories brim** with life. Both urgent and tender, full of a wisdom which makes a space for metamorphosis in the face of complexity and pain, these remarkable stories speak to the burning world. McBride has found for herself a language that is poetic, resonant, and full of care.

—Deryn Rees-Jones, poet, *Hôtel Amour* and T. S. Eliot Prize shortlisted *Erato* (Seren Books)

# BIRDS ARE LIARS

## & Other Stories

## Bernadette McBride

SPUYTEN DUYVIL
*New York City*

*For Rosalita and Cormac,*
*who make the end times new, our love is eternal.*

BIRDS ARE LIARS

Don't believe, my coat,
What the birds are saying;
You're the only one I confide in.
Don't be taken in: Birds tell
This same lie every spring.
Don't believe them, my coat, don't.
    —Orhan Veli Kanık
    Translated from the Turkish

# Birds are Liars

Church bells don't quit the day he leaves. Bellringing practice, perhaps. Or for love or for death.

Who knows. But the bell ringer rings on and on until surely their hands must be tired and their wrists aching from all that yanking on the ropes. Maybe, they take it in turns with another to carry on this physical burden of creating that sound which surely no hearing soul can ignore for miles around. Yet inside, for the bell ringer or ringers, the sound is something different, like listening to a heart murmur through a stethoscope.

He has lifted off.

On her PC, an open window shows a flight tracker. Outside, a bird flies too far away to make out, yet still visible. She decides to write down this story before he lands and then burn the book. Glancing up, she sees that at one hundred fifty-five kilometres into the journey to Istanbul, through the window to his left, the Lincolnshire Wolds are in his eyeline, if he knew. Grass and clouds are ubiquitous. In the opposite direction, a plane from New York passes by on its way to Frankfurt. Crossing the same Wolds as he does. Flying directly over Somersby, over Lord Tennyson's babbling brook, if they knew.

She knows she must type fast.

Bells are still beating at either end of Hope Street. A plane's left-behind lines come into view where the Gothic cathedral's top stops. She is thinking of how she is sick of planes—of what it takes to escape, but to still take your head with you, like her mother said, only to have it crammed into a small airless-winged capsule.

To breathe in and out.

God knows what, for two hours or more. Just to come back to it all. Bag carousel, and around they go. Passport control and around they go. She has always wanted stamps, and now she has got what she wanted. But they are outside. Burgundy passport beaten black and blue in a stampede for control of—

An inky bruise of a stamp documents her last escape: 0.605 t of CO2, including return. She tries hard to feel something like shame, or as the Swedes say, *Flygskam*. Tells herself it is just for now. Because moving through the sky means moving at least. Of course, the pain will still come.

She understands this only too well.

But who is judging Prince Wills or Lizzo?

The contrail in the sky fades. She can only see two small puffs now at its tail end, like candy floss in the bottom of a child's bag at the fairground. She imagines the wings finally touching down on the other side.

How will he feel?

She hears the words of the poet Orhan Veli in her ear and writes them to him: *The bells of water-carriers unceasingly ring; I am listening to Istanbul, intent, my eyes closed.*

Presses send.

Glancing up, the open flight tracker tells her he is suspended.

*One tick.*


She knew Orhan long before she knew him. Poems about birds who lie, and a woman encouraged to wear lipstick to an ice-cream parlour at promenade time. She thinks she could have loved Orhan, too, in a different lifetime.

Perhaps more.

It was a terrible end for Orhan after the fall of *Yaprak*, and it was folded. He came home, listened to Istanbul, and then left for Ankara. Everybody needs a holiday. A hole in the street had been dug by municipality workers, and the pain didn't seem too much at first. The doctors looked, not hard enough. The damage was all in his head, so they said. An aneurysm. They guessed at first that the poison seeping for so long in his veins had burst him star yellow.

The fall doesn't always show the fall.

She supposes we are all fallible, and this is what gets us in the end. The screen says he is in transit over the grey wiggles of the North Sea, past Amsterdam and the A7 motorway, where cars cruise below like sugar-laden ants, past The Hague and lands where people and animals were hunted, bypassing the King's palace and international justice.

*It is hard to describe,* he says, sniffing her neck again for good measure. Inhaling deeply. Almost at the bottom of her neck, moving his nose from the nape now and then around to the front. Down to the collarbone. Someone once told her in a nightclub that she had the neck of a swan. *It is like innocence.* He decides out loud.

She smiles.

They are on the couch, close, talking about poetry. But decide to move to the bed. He wants to rest his head on her petite breast and explain to her how some things are lost in translation. But he cannot find the right words. They were talking about Orhan's poem 'I Am Not Far'. The lines where he writes, *Your eyes shall know to look, I am in your looks.* She only has the English translation of Orhan's collected works. He says, *It does not translate.* In broken English, he tells her that her version is *not trustable.*

The plane is delayed. She now has four and a half hours instead of four. She starts writing at the sound of the next first bell chime on the street outside. Like moving off at the sound of a starter pistol, signifying the beginning of a track race.

And her hand moves.

He sits on the other side of his small, rented couch after changing from his restaurant clothes. Turns to her. *What if there's a war? What if the world sets on fire? Or the oceans between us drown everything that separates us, and we don't see each other waving until our hands disappear from view?*

That kind of thing.

She shrugs as though to offer reassurance, but it looks like a taunt.

After the couch conversation. She passes on a nugget from her old boss, *Relationships are like battleships, made for sinking.* Translation issues aside, *Interesting,* he responds and means it. She never understood what it meant herself, other than, *I want to fuck you behind my wife's back,* but at the same time, she understood exactly. The weight of it. And really, you have to consider, if things do ever float back up, how resurrectable are they? Bits of soiled nonbiodegradable plastic or a missing foot in a Nike. Who did the throwing, who remembers what was lost, and which part belonged to whom?

The lighted window shows him in the air over a small town now in Germany, Bad Lausick, and its spirits rise up from the cemetery of St. Kilian-Kirche, those lost in the Thirty Years' War and the plague. They rise. Meet the vapours of his path: carbon dioxide, sulphate and soot, and then keep on rising, up, up, away.

She had felt sad reading that Orhan was a drunk and a womaniser. Similar to hearing her childhood idol, Enid Blyton, neglected her own children to give readings to other children in her family home because that was what gave her validation. A people pedestal is her favourite object it seems, and she just has to hope that they won't fall off. They need to prove they are bad first before she will believe that they are not good. Case in point: When his dear comrade Nazim was imprisoned, Orhan held a hunger strike for three long days, and when his friends needed money for their shared literary magazine, he sold the coat off his own back. He had been a man who would sell the coat off his own back for those he loved. Yet Orhan had written in his poem, *Don't believe, my coat, What the birds are saying; You're the only one I confide in.* Orhan saved one friend and yet betrayed his only confidant.

It can't be proven he is bad enough to be sunk, but yes, he was bad in many ways.

The man beachcombs. He likes this sea. He did not care for the others, sneered at them, in fact. Said they were not real seas, as though natural science could be disputed by beauty or a perceived lack of purity, or both. She said at the time, *This one's a blue flag, actually.* Now, he finds a few coins and places them in his old overcoat pocket. He has been hungry for so long. Elsewhere, in a thickset wood, she climbs a tree and reaches out for something she wants. Needs. Arms outstretched towards the redness, she has waited for so long for this first frost to break.

*Snap.*

Goes the branch.

*Crunch.*

Goes the seaweed.

She moves a foot left; he moves a foot right.

Both *falling.*

Catches herself on a lower branch, a thorn snags her little finger, and there is a trickle of blood, she squeezes, and it drops down.

Lands.

Drips onto and down over his knee, red stain on his trousers.

Seaweed slippery.

Both up again.

He gathers by sea. She gathers by wood. Plucked rosehips to her basket, seashells to his overcoat pocket that whistle and howl inside.

She notices a flicker on the screen. The plane graphic shows he is getting further away from her. Over Brno-střed, Czechia, the city's people climb the observation tower and look up, spot a plane flying overhead, appearing to look down at them—like two children each looking through one circular open end of a long cardboard tube—exchanging a fleeting intimacy. Outside of them, the city's quirky astronomical clock tells of the timing and movement of celestial bodies.

There is a war. Two or three of them, in fact. Fires are spread all about; some are wild, some managed. Sea levels rise and start to swallow but then opt to spit out. Some people can't say out loud their *goodbyes,* even if they hate goodbyes, but would happily say their farewells anyway.

If only they could turn back time.

Bargains are made over and over. For the sake of— Stop. No, this isn't what really happens. Well, it is a bit like that, but all in a jumble of micro happenings and kaleidoscopic demise. Nobody can see far enough into oceans and out through the other sides to witness others' sufferings, and so they carry on.

He walks along the beach in Antalya with his beautiful wife and a young baby who looks just like him. His face still shows dimples when he smiles. They happen across a bottle stuck in the shore, glistening, mid-incoming turquoise waves.

This sea is real.

His beautiful wife is excited, wants to break open the bottle, sees the sun-faded message inside, and it is only getting hotter. *Leave it,* he says. *Why?* A silver-grey rock covered with molluscs is already at its side.

Shattered shards.

The baby cries.

He can't look.

Two children walk along a coastline. Bitter and cold amongst ironmen. Writing a letter to the future. Wind turbines wrestle lines from their hands during this writing and whilst trying to fold voices into a glass bottle before sealing them. Faces serious about what this message in a bottle might become. Every time they throw the bottle in, it keeps swimming back. Or some other young bather catches it in excitement and mistakenly thinks the past has caught up with the present. Finally, a tall man who is a strong swimmer, strides far out. He has the throw of a discus player, and it sets sail into the distance until they can no longer see.

Once grown, they have to wait too long, and they forget about waiting to see if anyone will find and bother to reply to their documented lives with their mother and all that they were. They decide some messages don't get through or don't want to be resurrected. It is a shame because they had imagined themselves on television twenty years or so from that first throwing and rethrowing. And the finder had been pleased to know about them and see how their lives had panned out.

The flight tracker has almost finished.
After he lands, she will know nothing of his path and instead imagine all his moments from then on. The green

tips of Çilingoz Nature Park in the rural Çatalca district of Istanbul foreshadow his landing into the heart of the city, and already he is *listening to Istanbul—intent, with his eyes closed,* ear pressed hard against a cold plastic pane.

Flight mode off.

*Two ticks.*


The sun is bad for ageing, but she isn't ageing too badly considering her relocation. The waves still come at odd times these days, these years, but she rides them. She smashes together a recipe for the lines:


*Sixty rosehips, dry, thorns removed.*

*Bruise with a makeshift mortar to force the seeds to bleed their medicinal hearts out in with the olive oil.*

*Bake on a low heat for a long time, without adding heat to the other heat in the house, if you can.*

*Remove and let it all settle in a dark place.*


On a dusty terrace overlooking Tuscan hills, she taps words into a device on a nineties writing desk. She prefers to work and write al fresco. To let the air flow into her and out of her. Acclimatise each day to however she encounters her environment. This is the best way to handle things. She is alone each day, save for the sparrows, who are also vulnerable and on the Red List. They fly back and forth between the umbrella pine trees and the terrace railing and feign interest in the removed rosehip leaves and body parts she leaves strewn in a wicker basket there.

*Once settled, remove from the dark and strain through a cheesecloth or, in its absence, an old pair of tights.*

*Massage deeply into vertical lines above lips from where face-plumping food has become harder to access if you don't want to leave your valley.*

A female sparrow makes chattering noises and, too, feels the absence of the plumping foodstuffs; has young back at the nest. She looks up and mimics the noise back at the sparrow. She feels another wave. Keeps very still. Sparrow's breast pauses too. Both their next exhalations are suspended in the air. Eyes are locked. Waiting for it to pass. An edge refuses to fully recede.

She holds her hand out with an offering, two plump rosehips full of seeds missed from pulverisation. Sparrow lands on her hand and has pale brown markings, but darker than those of her male counterpart. Soft beak meets the lines of her upturned palm just in the exact place, in the line break, where fortune tellers' faces always falter. Sparrow takes the seeds and flies away, not looking back.

Typing becomes faster on the device; presses send to her own far-flung young.

*Will it be ok?* She cries after sparrow, after the receding flight path, like calling after slowly disappearing plane plumes. Hears a short, sharp *shirp* in response, a mother's reassurance.

Birds are liars.

# FOR THE MAN WHO DIED
## IN THE WOOD

*Learning to make marks using hammers,* the sentence runs through a thin paper photo collage displayed on a fridge. Not the one where the body was taken. It's a tall silver economy fridge belonging to the mother of the little boy who had learnt to make many marks with his friends in the wood. The woman can't unsee the memory, as a fluorescent yellow border around the words makes the letters go *pop*.

Tree falls. Man falls. And after the storm, they never went back. The mother wonders about the dog who waited by the man's side. The gates on all four corners of the wood stay locked, and the entrance pathways become overgrown. Nature flourished and perished. Habitats for birds undisturbed, a call to a wood dead but for their own kind, and the squirrels and the things that crawl beneath.

The singing became louder as the days blurred, Winter turned to Spring, and passers-by trailed the streets around the perimeter of the wood, pressing their ears to the cold, black railings which lined its borders. Some half inclined to jump over to hear more, but they daren't.

Food scarce.

Nothing dropped, littered, or left, even out of kindness. Muddied warning signs on all entry points forbidding any human, good, bad, or in-between, to come in. Someone from the government holds the key and comes by once or twice to check for danger. Again. Leaves.

The mother opens the fridge to get some milk, and free, happy faces jump at her from the collage. That was the last time the birds saw the children. Jumping off logs in high-vis vests, paid for engagement with nature. Escaping the city's fumes on the nursery bus. Dimpled hands clasped together, holding s'mores over a fire, barely warm hot cocoa dripping from their mouths, running a rivulet over their chins and down their soft necks.

The note on the wood's gates simply says, *There is no time or date given for this site to reopen.* What does that mean? Perhaps it will be left untouched like some shrine. But unlike a bedroom with dust gathering and all the stillness that offers sameness, life will carry on. The fungus will grow on trees. Creatures will find a way to feed or leave. New birds will come. Some things, though, will be unmoved: a lost red Wellington boot, tree branches gathered and bent over in a child's prayer for protection, fashioned into a triangle roof.

And what of the storm whose passage across Europe was at the beginning of all this? Ciara. The Irish feminine version of Ciarán, meaning black, or little black one. Funny how the gale was so drawn to a wood going by the name of Black Wood, as though two magnets of darkness, unable to resist the pull of the other, and then *snap*. Still, the fridge magnet holds up hope on a piece of paper.

High winds and rain that fell and rose around car wheels, and the people stayed home. When the tree fell, and the man fell, a storm had just passed. But tree roots were weakened, which, according to the locals who spoke up after, were long rotten and unstable. And they were a gift, so they were, left to the people of the city by wealthy landowners a long time ago. At least four to five pairs of great spotted woodpeckers recorded in the wood once, dining out and drumming ruffles on a feast of deadwood. *Fwump-fwump, fwump-fwump,* they foraged, roosted, and nested, not interested in living trees like their sap-sucking neighbours.

Post-storm air with all its crispy cleanness, stillness, the kind asthmatics open their lungs up to. And so, the human had believed he was safe. What sound does a tree make when falling? They say a dog can hear nearly twice as many frequencies as a human from four times the distance that they can sniff things out, given training: an oncoming seizure in an epileptic or a virus. If he had lived to tell the tale, the man might have said, *The sound is a bit like fireworks going off, at the start.*

The dog was by the man's side until help came too late.


They go by the Black Wood most days, and the boy looks out the car window. If he remembers, he doesn't say. The mother is tempted to climb over the gates in the moments she has alone. She's not afraid of being killed by trees. Perhaps she is worried about being caught, being a rule breaker, or seeing something she can't unsee. But she wonders about the wood all the time.

A battle ensues with the freezer door below the fridge, long days lead to many visits, and small, hungry children do not wish to hear the word *later.* The mother removes her knee. Looking at the photo collage above, the top grid shows a trio of photos of her son alone. In a series of three photos, he holds what appears to be a white flag fastened onto a long stick, at full mast, at half mast, then lowered. Once laid on the ground, with a wooden mallet, tongue out in concentration, he makes a series of markings with material from the earth.

The mother always dreams at night, strange, startling dreams hard to wake from. But this time, they take flight. In the dark, she moves, pillows and books falling. She goes back to earlier in the year and is a high-flying windstorm. She does not want to cause devastation, just to see this locked-in world. At her fastest—one hundred and thirty-six miles per hour—her form passes by Cap Corse on the most northern point of Corsica. So fast the little boats in the harbour shake and cry, and early Christian settlements are almost excavated.

Warnings spread across Europe.

She is a tailwind that sees a world record broken for the fastest-ever flight time from New York to London Heathrow in just four hours and fifty-six minutes. In any form, she never imagined she could become a world record-breaker. Next, she takes in Northern Scotland and Norway, flying right through the auroras as though a ghost. Blowing worse through her beloved Ireland, which she misses so. In visiting, she takes away the lives of others along the path to somewhere else. In Hampshire, an Irishman dies when another falling tree hits his car. Described as well-loved. A woman and her two daughters are buried as she takes the roof off a ski rental shop in Poland. She wants to see the works of Rafał Olbiński at the Polish Museum in Rapperswil, but realises it's in Sweden after all. Like a demonic drone, her form passes through the Swedish Alps and inland rivers, searching for art. A man's boat capsizes, and he drowns, hands waving until the tips sink. As she dreams, above the fireplace in her room sits a large print by Olbiński she got in another lifetime at an art market in East Berlin. She gave it away once because she came to dislike the man who bought it for her as a gift. But she realised the art meant more than the man, and so she got it back. In the white frame, another woman sits on a chair in a red dress and watches over her, long legs stretching right up to the moon, which she uses as a footstool. A cool lake is surrounded by evergreens and props up a midnight-blue sky. It's the surrealist poster Olbiński was commissioned to make for a Polish theatre production of Cinderella. But the woman is depicted as barefoot and uninterested in glass slippers.

Stars.

Flying now through a wood she recognises, and night gives way to day. Her powers lessen, and there is silence. Footsteps can be heard gently treading through a mossy morning carpet and the pitter-patter of non-human feet.

Then, the falling and what comes after, she doesn't know, as her form evaporates. More light footsteps, and her eyes open.

She checks the death rates and prepares to face the dishes.

Hatchlings hear something they don't recognise: a form unfamiliar in all their newborn hours. They nestle closer to their mother, burrowing deeper into the twigged bed and listen to hear if the thing passes. Their eyes have not yet opened. It moves below. It's climbing. Their mother's breast trembles against them, and her heartbeat is all a *flutter-flutter.* It's not so easy for her to fly away and leave them, but she would as they would their young. Loud noises and something else follow, which almost dislodges them, but they are stuck safe with their mother's glue. The thing has a hammer, makes markings; synthetic colours left on the oak that stands them tall. Feathers would have pierced through their skin as they learnt to perch and walk, to open their eyes. Catching mealworms in tiny open beaks. It's a long way to fall with your eyes closed, so new, naked, and blind. Nothing will save them. No one passes there now aside from the man from the government and his marksman.

The boy sees their eyes watching him, all sitting apart.

Some smile, others frown, no bother, he can't see beyond the things. Jesus is on a stained-glass window high up, looking down at him. *I'm scared,* he says to his mother. *Look at the window,* she says. *What colours do you see? Red, blue, green, and... some gold.* He knew Jesus only as a toy doll lying in the hay, that time he was a sheep with black stockings. He says he wants to leave, to go home. His mother doesn't seem to hear, so he says it louder. A song plays, and no one sings, aside from one man, who follows along beneath his breath, moist material moving.

*Can I pick this stick up? Can I bring it home? No, no.* His hands are peeling. The more the boy touches, the more they peel. He's hungry all the time, though he's left to eat as much as he likes.

His cars are the same colours as Jesus in the high window in the place where music played without voices. He looks through the sunblind in the car window and sees the gates with tall grass and bushes climbing up high over the tops like Spiderman. And he knows they will drive past be-cause they always do and never stop.

He is learning that some things can't go back.

The boy remembers the hammers and the marks, and the colours from the earth, and the radio in the nursery bus on the way, and how he had heard his daddy's voice. *That's your daddy.* They told him he was talking about something important, and the boy felt surprised and happy to hear him as they were leaving the city.

A black, thick road runs across the length now. Below, some say there's a grave for the wood and all that it was, to the boy, to the man and his dog, to the birds and their fallen, splayed hatchlings. And the woman who wondered. A tarmac roundabout is a compass pointing to the old gates: North, East, South, West, each entry now replaced with an exit. The great paired woodpeckers are long gone, their *fwump-fwump* dying out with the sounds of workmen's tools drilling into the soil as if they were one of the same kinds, exposing cavities for goods.

There was singing again, though, and new sounds, and the sirens stopped. But it took a long time. As long as it takes for a woodland to rot right down to its roots and for all life to up and leave and return just to check and then leave for good. Then to be pushed right down in the ground with the lid closed over like a forest in a coffin, or a greenhouse without windows.

On the former North gate, now the first roundabout exit, there are a bunch of flowers left.

*Dedicated to all those who lost their lives or suffered due to COVID-19*

# THE BATTLE OF SKIBB

*They set my roof on fire with cursed English spleen*
*And that's another reason that I left old Skibbereen.*
  "Revenge for Skibbereen" (Famine Ballad, c.1880)


You walk into a second-hand bookshop. It is bent back against the curve of the River Lee. It runs through Cork City. You are a Cork girl, through and—well, in your blood you are, *I am in my blood*, you self-affirm, swinging open the shop door. You enter. In your head, you expect it to be like a scene from a Spaghetti Western, glass doors pushing forward like double saloon doors. Once inside, you imagine local book punters stopping—like the piano and girl dancing on a bar—to stare. In your ear, you hear the classic Western whistle as you go in, but in this case, it is mixed with a little bit of Irish flute, a Transatlantic call. It has been a long time. None of this happens. For one, the bookshop is too empty to cause a stir.

There is an air of something, though, and paperbacks rustle. You are looking for *something*. You expect to be asked. But the girl on the till doesn't say, *Are you looking for some-*

*thing?*—in the timeframe you expect. The girl is busy with a young man. You are a *blow-in*. He is a *local*. He writes things down on a notepad, listing and listing. He really *needs* the bookseller to find what he writes down. Perhaps he is neurodivergent or simply has an insatiable physical and mental urge to acquire those authors. Some deep yearning within that keeps him awake at night, and if he does not get those names, he will combust. He will die of wonder from their unfinding. He writes down the possible dates they might come in so he can stake out the shop. The girl cannot say when for sure. *And so, I'll be in next week, so I will,* he tells her. The bookseller looks up at him one last time. Holds his gaze. Her eyes tell him that the situation is in safe hands, and then she simply smiles. A tight smile. But one hundred percent trustable as far as book ordering and acquiring is within her power.

You observe all of this stealthily in ten seconds or so, and then you turn on your heels towards the second-hand short fiction section. The book is standing up on the lower shelves, to the left, out of the way. The one drawing you to it, with its faded off-white and blue dusty paperback cover. Its title promises to take you down a road of sorts, *The Road to the Shore*, by Michael MacLaverty. You set your shoulders back. You prepare to make contact with your siren. Step forward. Step closer. Your hands are on it. It's off the shelf. It is in the air. Your hands are widening its pages, opening it like a bird with its wings out and about to take flight. You inhale the distinct perfume of its past. You hear something drop out onto the floor. A message. You look around to see if anybody saw you or it. No one did, or you don't think so. You look about you again and stoop down to retrieve it. On your face, you try to say, *Oh, my bus ticket*, or *Oh, my old receipt*, casual-like. You don't want the bookseller to notice and try to interfere with this found treasure. Take it away, perhaps. You pretend to read the book, but you have the thing that fell out back up there, stuck inside it. With your forefinger, you firmly hold it against the book's pages, so it doesn't fall to the floor again as you examine it. You simultaneously read a line of MacLaverty's prose: *She rubbed her wrinkled hands together and looked out at the thrushes.* And then, print from the found thing: *$27.00*—words and numbers merge and then divide. It is a ticket from somewhere to somewhere else from the year 1999. And there is a passenger's name, but it is faded. The ticket serial number blocks out some of the surname and makes it even harder to read. It is an Amtrak train ticket from Portland, Oregon, to Seattle, Washington, in the United States.

You check the publication details: an Irish publisher, Poolbeg Press, from near Dublin, and the book was printed in 1976. On the blue and white front cover is a picture of a lighthouse, and all about it there are boats, men, and birds, running and flying away, high into the sky. You wonder what they are all trying to escape from and where to. You don't think this copy of *The Road to the Shore, and other stories* by Michael MacLaverty, has been opened in many years, perhaps since 1999, when the reader was reading it on the train from Portland to Seattle. The faded ticket would have slipped out by now, like it just did for you. The ticket's texture is ultra-silky; any pulpy paper fibres long worn smooth by the past, and it is only held firm now by the weight of a book which stays closed and unread. And so, a story had stayed locked within a story.

You try to think about it. You close your eyes and *summon*. The year is 1999; you are a would-be person sitting on a stateside train travelling from Portland to Seattle. You have a book with you, a collection of short stories by the Irish writer Michael MacLaverty, and this book was published in 1976 in Ireland. You could be *anybody of any descent*. But the book came back here to Ireland from the US, so you guess this book was passed down through an Irish bloodline. It was made in Ireland. It left Ireland. Somehow, it crossed the Atlantic, but then it came back. On the train, from Portland to Seattle, as the would-be you passed by the Puget Sound, with views of the Northern Pacific Ocean through your would-be window, the book was at least twenty-three years old back then.

You imagine, you are a twenty-three-year-old Irish diaspora settled stateside after your great-great-great-grandparents emigrated there after escaping during the famine years, on a boat which passed by Fastnet Lighthouse along the coast of West Cork—the last teardrop of Ireland—and they settled, and it was hard, so hard, but they survived. And maybe your parents' parents, they flourished over there and worked and worked to save for their children's future, and one day they all flew home again—those who were still alive—to visit, and they were no longer dead. And maybe they picked up MacLaverty's book to take back to America as a reminder of how great Irish literature was, is. This was the seventies, and Bob Geldof was a scandal on *The Late Late Show* saying this, your, their, country *is a shithole*, people riling up about environmental issues—Carnsore Point and nuclear power—the Troubles, so much trouble, the petrol strikes, and the fight, the fight for women's rights, and then in 1976, the state of emergency in the Republic, legally in force since 1939, lifted, but did it? U2 formed a secondary school band, and the Rooney Prize for literature was launched, all in the same year MacLaverty published this book.

Perhaps now, you imagine your would-be self in 1976 as a new baby—if you were the person who had owned that train ticket—and your parents took you *back home to Ireland,* and it was when you were older that you were on that train in 1999, from Portland to Seattle. Old enough to read and try to impress the American girls in the opposite seats, with your swept-back dark hair and blue-grey Irish inherited eyes against pale skin and the freckles across your nose and broadening jawline becoming a constellation. But your would-be father, maybe he grew sick and homesick in his heart for Ireland, even though he only knew it in spirit, and he left, and he took the book he loaned you on that 1999 train journey with him, and then he died. And would-be you went back to Ireland after that and cleared his house, and you forgot the book you once read as a young man on the way to Seattle to make a stand on the day your life was changed forever.

And your would-be self barely remembered the train ticket inside a book from that day, as you dropped it off in a box with other books swept from the shelf without looking—dealing with the affairs of the dead is heavy and hard and time-consuming—and some things are best forgotten.

You come back to the present moment, to you, *you*, not the would-be bearer of the found train ticket. You sidle the ticket away inside your handbag, it is tote style, and you let it drop in soundlessly whilst looking straight ahead. You place the second-hand copy of *The Road to the Shore*, by Michael MacLaverty, on the till desk to pay. The bookseller doesn't say much, just the price, *€4.50, please*. She can tell you have had no trouble finding what it is you have been looking for. Once outside, the air from the river hits your face and pulls you from your dream. You drop the book into the bag as you did with the ticket, like dropping a body into a pit.

You have a bus to catch.

You decide that the 237 bus from Cork City to West Cork

is a special kind of people carrier. Only those who have ever caught the 237 bus can understand. It is coming up to the end of August, and it is unseasonably hot. At Clonakilty, the bus stops, and four men in about their sixties get on wearing Christmas hats. They are drunk and gather about a woman sitting opposite you, who, it turns out, was at the wedding recently of a cousin of the lady whose hotel you are to stay at. The men give her all their marital details without being asked; they are widowed, married, divorced, have a second wife, and so on. In return, she offers them unspoken counsel via mystical language about the weather and sighs heavily when they get off. One of them, suspiciously, had asked you what you were doing on the 237 and where you were going and where you were from. You said you were getting off at the last stop of this stretch of bus route along West Cork at the old council offices in Skibbereen. They asked you your reason for going, and their eyes seemed suddenly sober. The lights on their Christmas hats stopped flashing ridiculously, if only briefly. *My family was from there.* They replied: *Well, if that's so, then you should know, they don't call it Skibbereen; they call it Skibb.* Your home for the night in Skibb is right opposite the bus stop and the old council offices. You stare at the sign outside and admire the proprietor's ingenuity in combining the functions of their dwellings and their services during these hard times. *McCarthy's Bed and Breakfast* is on the left-hand side of the sign; *McCarthy's Wills and Life Insurance* is on the right-hand side of the sign.

You wonder about this unashamed reminder of mortality, positioned alongside the offering of retreat, temporary residence, or a holiday or change from one's life. Does the reminder that one day their lives will be left behind sour the guests' moods or spur them on to make the most of their trip? You think about it a little. But not too much, you understand, that people have to make ends meet. You are hungry, and you decide to walk to the town's main large family-run supermarket for supplies. You came to this supermarket the last two times, and though that was a long time ago, you are quite sure you recognise the people standing around you. Two ladies with identical purple-hued grey hair talk in conspiratorial tones together by the cheese counter; it is like déjà vu. Or maybe they just come here every day, now, and have been doing so since then. Since you were last here.

The cheese prices have gone up.

You will have a nice little bottle of wine and picnic tea for one in your room and then go for an evening walk to get some air. Afterwards, you will come back to your room and prepare your family history documents for searching the next day at the famine museum and its adjoining family history centre. Your family name was McCarthy; the family historian on the phone, who arranged your appointment, explained that in this town, everyone was called McCarthy at some point. It was her job to dissect which sects of the McCarthy clan. You walk down Market Street, and you imagine your great-grandmother, something or other, buying groceries along here before getting back to all the children, having left some of the older ones in charge. Or maybe she would take her time, savouring the peace amid the hustle and bustle of Market Street as it was. You wonder what it would be like to be a woman with little means and at the mercy of a man, more so back then than now. You think about the history of these streets, *The Siege of Skibbereen* in the twenties, between the IRA and the Free State Army, you carry your inflated cheese in a bag and walk past the spot, just past North Street at Windmill Rock, where an IRA man, a young McCarthy, was shot, his lit cigarette giving him away. A fisherman-turned-soldier, he knew all about the dangers of the sea and bait. You think about your own great-grandfather and his flitting between the IRA and the

British Army; he had always cast his net wide, but he had been careful to cover his tracks.

Back at the hotel, the room begins to feel a little like a prison cell. You have a sudden sense of not belonging *any-where*—you start to panic—but you remember, you have been drawn to this place, back to Skibb.

The nice little bottle of wine becomes a nice big bottle of wine, and you go out walking. You take some air. You walk along the river, and you feel as though you are retracing footsteps of whose you are unsure, but you keep walking. You want to see where the famine and family history centre is before your appointment in the morning. You don't want to get lost, to miss your appointment, or miss your turn. The town feels so sleepy, and the buses idle past off-kilter with the timetable, but you have a feeling that, when it comes to matters of blood, this town will expect perfect punctuality because too much blood has been unaccounted for already. You see it, the heritage centre, place marking it in your mind as you carry on walking.

You end up walking further along the river. You ex-change evening pleasantries with a heron; its wings agape to dissipate the air, the evening is warm, the temperature is middle-of-the-day-Spanish-heat, from the early noughties girls' holidays you once had. The bottle of wine heats up the insides of your veins and makes your face, your whole body, glow. You become aware of the water close to your feet. If you were to take a small step to the right, you'd fall right in and drown. *Probably.* You try to steer your feet to the left; your feet are like a two-year-old who won't walk in the shop without tugging directions on the reins. You try to cajole them with a promise of a sweet at the end. You cross a bridge across the river, holding the sides firmly like a pensioner with a Zimmer frame. You want to get onto the main road, the N71, to see if you can find a bus to take you back to your hotel. You can't walk back, not now. Your head is hot and swirling. You need to lie down. You make it. You are on the other side of the river now, across the main road, but no buses come. You wait, and you wait. Your eyes are closing. Over a drystone wall, you spot some crosses and a lonely wooden bench. You decide to keep the bench company. Your mind is jumbled, and it can't make sense of where the gate to this place might be, so you start climbing over the stone wall. It feels quite unstable, not unlike yourself, but you manage it.

You sit down on the bench, and all of a sudden, you are

very thirsty. Your throat feels like it has swallowed sawdust. The red wine, although plentiful, was not hydrating, it seems. You scramble about in your Mary Poppins bag, searching for water. You find a bottle, but it is empty. You spot a tap across the crosses; it must be for watering plants and cleaning the graves, maybe, you think. Then you realise, for the first time, that you are in a cemetery, and on filling up your water at the faucet in the empty bottle, you look up and spot a sign on one of four stones positioned close together. It reads:

*PAUSE AND YOU CAN ALMOST HEAR THE SOUNDS*
*ECHO DOWN THE AGES*
*THE CREAK OF THE BURIAL CART*
*THE RATTLE OF THE HINGED-COFFIN DOOR*
*THE SIGH OF SPADE ON EARTH*
*NOW AND AGAIN*
*ALL DAY LONG*

You are beginning to sober up. You realise you are no better than the men on the 237 in Christmas hats. But this is what West Cork will do to a person. You tell yourself this. You realise you are at the burial site where over ten thousand people were buried during the famine years in unmarked mass graves. You read about this place when you were doing your homework before this visit. The night all of a sudden becomes very still, and the wine in your veins begins to cool. You are a stranger in this place, on the surface, and there is no one else to be seen as far as your blurry eyes can see. You sit very still and think about the bodies, about the souls beneath your feet. And about how they have been alone for so long, yet all together. But without the dignity they deserved.

You wonder if any of your own are buried here, well, your own by blood. Perhaps some great-great-great-grandmother lies below. Maybe she has your eyes and you hers. She might have a look of you, and you a look of her. You really need a female elder right now. You imagine yourself and her sitting together on the bench in this moment. Talking and drinking tea. You imagine it was her footsteps you felt a force to follow here. You close your eyes, and when you open them, she is sitting right there with you. She holds your hand. You hold hers. You tell her *everything*. She tells you *everything*, about *An Drochshaol,* the bad life. About the story of the three-year-old boy Tom Guerin, who was thrown in the pit beside her but, on the second day, buried alive, rose again, and lived to be a sixty-five-year-old beggar-poet, who wrote: *I rose from the dead in the year '48 / When a grave at the Abbey had near been my fate,* in order to persuade the Guardians of the Workhouse to buy him a pair of new shoes.

You think about all the trapped stories in the world. You both take the tea, you and your female forebear, sipping it slowly, sip by sip, all the while you are looking at each other, you are like a mirror to the future, she is a mirror to the past, and at the same time, you are a mirror of one another. You are the same woman. You start to ask her questions because you know that tomorrow, the woman in the family history centre can only tell you so much. You know that the stories of the McCarthys, in particular, the stories of Mary McCarthys, will be hard for her to trace. Not because of the high occurrence of that common recorded name but because of the common experiences of shared loss and grief all those Marys lived through until their names became paper or soil, written or lost. You ask Mary about all the Marys you heard of through family folklore; the baby Mary who was scalded to death with boiling water from a tin bath by the fire, whose mother Mary hadn't realised, and then she was tried for her crimes. The grandmother, Mary, who had more children than most and kept on producing double at a time through the laying of two eggs a cycle, yet she could not produce yolk eggs for their sustenance, and so they were sent to the brothers and sisters of the church. And some of them were hurt, and some of them never came back, and some of them decided to extinguish their own memories for good because flashbacks are more reliable than paper. You had read that a McCarthy's house was found just outside Skibb, with a British burn layer to the ground, and two tiny ceramic doll heads were left behind, scorched and with their clothes missing. You ask her, *Was that us?* And she says, *No, it was another McCarthy, but at the same time, It was all of us.*

You ask her about Mother Mary, *Does she still believe?* And she tells you, *I am her.* You wonder, did she die with a fever? She seems confused now; her eyes are disoriented. Is she the Virgin Mary, or was she one of the bodies tipped in the dead of night into the pit, unshrouded, by a loved one who could not afford to be seen with the black death upon or near them, for fear of loss of work amid such fragility and blight. You think about the masks and the gloves and the time you stopped your own child picking daisies after watching on TV the helicopters in Europe dropping dis-infectants onto the land. And the land burned and insects died, until they realised that people were the main problem. The old shame and fear had returned and carried over on the breeze of the Irish Sea, the arm of the North Atlantic Ocean separating Ireland from Great Britain. Again, the dead could not be held when they needed to be held. Again, governments were unaccountable.

This Mary sitting opposite you needs to finally rest, Virgin Mother or not. You hug her goodbye, folding her woollen shawl about her shoulders. Her time is cold, yours is hot, and in return, she loosens your own jacket for you. You don't want to say goodbye.

You admit defeat on the bus front and finally get hold of a local taxi driver who is willing to come out past teatime; as you wait, you pull out the other story again, with the printed train ticket from Portland to Seattle inside. The taxi is taking a while. You Google what happened on the day of the train ticket in Seattle in 1999. The search results tell you it was on the same day as the *Battle of Seattle*, the protests against the World Trade Organization and their new policies for economic globalisation. Young protestors travelled from other US cities and protested against the policies' potential impacts on free trade and the environment.

There was a riot. Some said protesters threw Molotov cocktails at the police, unwarranted. Some said the police beat the protestors for no good reason. A name from one of the headlines catches your eye, McCarthy, a young man who was arrested and wrongfully charged, only to wait years for redemption. You try to read the surname on the ticket again, but it is too late; it is too faded.

The taxi driver finally turns up forty minutes later. He says he had some trouble getting parts for his car from the producer in Northern Ireland, *Bloody Brexit*, he huffs, and drives you back to the place with the sign that reminds you of what it means to live and what it means to leave a life behind.

# WHITE HART

*'Tis the white stag, Fame, we're a-hunting, Bid the world's hounds come to horn!*

—Ezra Pound

A Police Report:

Case no: 10497

**Date:** Sunday, 26th September 2021

**Reporting officer:** D. Hatton

**Incident:** Shooting [euthanization] of a wild white deer in the Toxteth area

**Detail of event:**

Where did he come from? Nobody knows. A concerned member of the public was driving down Princes Avenue on their way to work when they noticed White Hart breaking into a canter just past the derelict Welsh Presbyterian Church. The early morning sun streamed through the church's missing roof tiles, casting a golden halo around his head and antlers. High up, on the church's wind-exposed eaves, nesting pigeons ruffled their feathers at the sight of this early morning omen. City council CCTV showed that White Hart had started his journey down Princes Avenue at the junction of Upper Parliament Street. Close-up footage revealed him reading the headlines outside Rialto News: *Amtrak train derails in Montana, killing three and injuring dozens,* as White Hart picked up pace.

He first crossed by the old Liverpool Queen Victoria District Nursing Association building, which bore a stony-faced Queen Victoria over its front door, shouting from either side of her head, from her lips, words cast in terracotta brick, *Nursing the poor in their own homes and in commemoration of the Queen's long and beneficent reign,* and yet, she had blocked aid to the Irish poor.

There were only two known relations of White Hart's fellow white fallow, in Ireland, in County Tyrone and County Cork. Where did he come from? Local officers had done their patrol rounds first thing, just ten minutes before the first call-in, and they had not noticed the animal, white as he was.

White Hart was considered very rare in the kingdom and lands he wandered; indeed, only a handful of sightings had been reported over the last few decades. A man named Eustace, who, whilst out hunting hares, on the Big Moor of the Peaks, just outside Sheffield, was said to have seen a vision between a stag's antlers as he cornered it, and then learnt that he would suffer. That was the last time.

Now, White Hart is moving faster down Princes Avenue in Toxteth, Liverpool. *Gallop, gallop*—past the Neo-Byzantine Greek Orthodox Church of St Nicholas—as though some ghostly *Marian* apparition, then outpacing the length of the still opulent Moorish revival synagogue. Next, looking out across the central boulevard towards the Kuumba Imani Millennium Centre and letting his eyes rest on the words: *Education is the most powerful weapon you can use to change the world,* with bold yellow and white lettering propped up by the shoulders of a green and black pop painted Nelson Mandela.

In the city streets White Hart traverses, there have been forty-three-gun shootings that year alone:

*Rat-tat-tat*

*Rat-tat-tat*

*Rat-tat-tat*

*Rat-tat-tat*

*Rat-tat-tat*

*Rat-tat-tat*

*Rat-tat-tat*

*Rat-tat-tat*

*Rat-tat-tat*

*Rat-tat-tat*

*Rat-tat-tat*

*Rat-tat-tat*

*Rat-tat-tat*

*Rat-tat-tat*

*Rat-tat-tat*

*Rat-tat-tat*

*Rat-tat-tat*

*Rat-tat-tat*

*Rat-tat-tat*

*Rat-tat-tat*

*Rat-tat-tat*

*Rat-tat-tat*

*Rat-tat-tat*

*Rat-tat-tat*

*Rat-tat-tat*

*Rat-tat-tat*

*Rat-tat-tat*

*Rat-tat-tat*

*Rat-tat-tat*

*Rat-tat-tat*

*Rat-tat-tat*

*Rat-tat-tat*

*Rat-tat-tat*

*Rat-tat-tat*

*Rat-tat-tat*

*Rat-tat-tat*

*Rat-tat-tat*

*Rat-tat-tat*

*Rat-tat-tat*

*Rat-tat-tat*

*Rat-tat-tat*

*Rat-tat-tat*

But law and order are always there to protect, and so White Hart carries on. Tasked with delivering a message written on a scroll rolled and hidden from first sight, but still tightly tied to White Hart's body. The day wakes up, and Princes Avenue cycle lane begins to fill, the fallow flies along past the houses of captains of industry and worship. White Hart's visual journey is interspersed by past and present echoes of prayer and signs too. On the side of a seated shelter running along the boulevard, red words sprayed in the memory of spilt blood spell out, *FUCK THE COPS!* On another sign outside a church garden, there is a manifesto: *COMMUNITY, HOPE, FAITH.* And just past the empty plinth and the slain ghost of the slavery-defender Huskisson, there is a newly planted sweet chestnut tree, its leaves growing all over the world, and a plaque reading: *Paths of peace, trees of knowledge, birds of freedom, leaves of hope.*

Many strange sights have been seen along that avenue; some turn a blind eye, some notice, and some stand up. Remonstrating with those tasked to maintain order. In the past, the stander-uppers had danced on milk floats with the stars of the night as fireballs in their hands. And stars they did shoot with as police officers approached, wishes being the throwers' only ammunition. In the second wave, in the eighties, a police vehicle was instructed to move about, just a little jig, enough to try and instil some controlled fear to help disperse the crowds, no more. A young black man was hit and killed upon contact with a patrol car, and the Rialto Ballroom blazed, and people retraced imaginary footsteps on an imaginary dance floor roof. Heels hot. Back then, since then, and now, many a boy has stood with their arms folded behind and wrists cuffed into a twist along that avenue, long limbs running down like the tree roots of the planes which crossed the middle of the tree-lined boulevard—strong and rooted—knowing from experience where to put their energy in rough weather.

A woman had been driving along Princes Avenue the week before and had noticed a young man held in a stop-and-search, in an expensive-looking coat, photographing flowers, with an expensive-looking camera. Primrose yellow lilies shook inside his lens but held themselves steady. This sight was more common, but no one stopped and reported it on their way to work.

White Hart stops momentarily to gather his bearings as he trots past the Welsh Presbyterian Church again, drawn back to his Celtic roots, and as White Hart looks up, a middle-aged woman in a clapped-out Ford Fiesta is kerb-crawling and videoing his every movement.

White Hart is ready to deliver the scroll; she must be the one, the receiver.

The scroll is a missile thrown through her open car window, and the middle-aged woman traces her fingers over the papyrus paper—and looks White Hart right in the eye—her time has come.

Within a minute, clips are uploaded to her social media, and White Hart has gone viral. The middle-aged woman smiles—Fame at last.

She takes off, scroll in one hand, phone in the other, and White Hart pricks up his ears. Antlers tilted at the sound of something alarming, dangerous, of trouble. To White Hart, it sounds something like, *wooooooOOOOoooooo, wooooooOOOOoooooo.*

The middle-aged woman has called.

White Hart freezes like an object frozen into a painting and stands still, an eternal aesthetic representation of his own place in folklore history. Passersby stop and sit along the boulevard's benches to view the new art sculpture found along Princes Avenue, and White Hart takes this seriously, lifting his chin and striking a pose: majestic.

*WooooooOOOOoooooo, wooooooOOOOoooooo,* the sound gets closer and becomes engulfed with the quickening of White Hart's heart; he is unable to turn off his ultrasonic hearing. At peace, he has the resting heart rate of a young male athlete, but as the *wooooooOOOOoooooo* gets closer, White Hart's pulse and bodily movements quicken along with the approaching beat of police officers' feet.

A lad on a scrambler, with a black hood pulled up high over his dark eyes, shouts out a warning to White Hart, *LID, THE FUCKING BIZZIES, RUN!* He whizzes on, front wheels up like Pegasus, his racer like a horse, and his grit, the wings that lift him up, up, away.

*Wooooo**OOOO**ooooo. Wooooo**OOOO**ooooo*—

White Hart makes haste.

**Action Taken:**

An animal welfare organisation advises officers on duty to let the animal alone, as it will most likely make its own way home down the Leeds and Liverpool Canal or the promenade. Still, those trying to maintain controlled fear cannot accept counsel from those in charge of welfare.

With each tranquiliser dart, White Hart's will to survive grows and grows until his aura is higher than the hundreds of years old planes growing down the middle of the avenue, and the boys in the black and white lapels reload. One arrow, two, three arrows, four, fiv—

*Schwoof Schwoof Schwoof Schwoof*

*Schwo—*

The last arrow misses its target and ricochets off a purple wheelie bin, and White Hart, though poisoned, takes his chance and leaps—

Towards the Welsh Streets. To the river.

White Hart is not afraid of death—in a way, all deer die before they really die—when their antlers are fully grown, and their velvet passes away, and so the deer buck rubs it off against a tree or other vegetation.

The smell of the river and its salt is getting closer to White Hart's nostrils, and though his legs are shaking from the poisoned arrows, he breaks into a long canter, the final stretch, and he's about to leap over the promenade railings—

*RAT-A-TAT-TAT*

White Hart is slain—

The River Mersey is a pool of grey now and mythical blood mixed in with the ancient steel smokes of Cammell Laird, and White Hart's body sinks down, down into its murky waters, and something in the sky catches the officers' eyes.

The officers look up.

Two figures are in the sky flying high over the river towards Cheshire; it is Pegasus; he has returned on his racer to save White Hart, who rides with him, now a fallow with wings which flew out of him the minute his spirit left his animal body on the last *–TAT*

On a bench along the river, a middle-aged woman is sitting in the sun and reading the weekly news on a scroll and happens to look up and wave at Pegasus and White Hart as they float past, and she smiles at them, a big, huge beam, and waves before her hand goes down to her pocket.

Within a minute, a police helicopter gives chase, *whrrr, whrrr, whrrr*—

The Cheshirean mediaeval Forests of Mara and Mondrem across the River Mersey are calling White Hart home, and he must fly faster— *whrrr, whrrr, whrrr* — Pegasus takes the chain of his Kyoketsu-Shoge knife and attaches it to White Hart's antlers and his bike's back bars and then revs his winged scrambler— *BRAAP*—

*Whrrr Whrrr*

*WHRRRR*—

Pegasus puts his foot down hard on his racer, *BRAAP, BRAAPPPP,* with White Hart under his wings, and now, they live under the laws of the forest.

# Washed Over

Teacher is retired from saying out loud what he knows, day after day, and often internally after hours. The chalk in hand, the blackboard pose, the passive faces, now no more. He is not done learning, though. Still hungry, he hunts for clues amongst fine yellow grains as time runs through an invisible hourglass. He has a new pose. Head hunched towards the sand like a shorebird searching for a morsel. Bill down. He is all mixed up with the sanderlings who scurry along the beach like clockwork toys, close to the water's edge, and are on the whole, as Teacher is, oblivious to close approach.

From a distance, some would say they are curious creatures. He with his ruler and camera, and old coat and hat, whatever the weather, and they, with their sand crab devouring mouths and bearing a plumage of spangled black, white, and rich rufous on heads, necks, and backs, right now. They work together in a perpetual game of wave chase. Receding waves leave behind soft wetness, and in one action, there is the snap of a camera, *wish-wash,* in another action, a bite of something. All with bicycling legs. Stopping frequently to pick over either food or the past. A regular birder has his hand out at them and bears witness.

Teacher unfurls himself; he has become entangled with wires and seaweed. Oh, what a retirement hobby. Some would say the merging of his body with past and present, the reshaping of the self, could be dangerous at his age. One wrongfooting could send him crashing over until he is ice and grey, like the sea before him. Ephemeral. A hip shattering onto shoal, bone amidst mollusc, if he was lucky. But creatures learn to live with risk when what it is they hunt enables them to carry on living.

It's getting closer now, time to turn back, one becomes monstrous, and for a second, it's a wall with a glass window, and he's looking at her through it. She smiles. He measures. She used to keep him company with this task of talekeeping, but then she started to forget the present. One day, she tried to use the length of a razor clam against the footprint of a child, to size it by shell. She wrote it down, *three-quarters of a razor fish shell*, and kept it. Through her, Teacher had been given a past he didn't have to work hard at preserving. To recall their lives for him was as simple as a blink, like holding a seashell against an ear and hearing the sea coming back, roaring. They'd had their time, but he couldn't let go.

In the early days, they had come across two sets of parallel footprints along the shore, sun-baked once as the shoreline moved, then exposed by the tide and coastal squeeze. The trail of a man about one hundred and eighty centimetres tall, and alongside him, the trail of a woman one hundred and seventy centimetres or so. And hand in hand, they had mirrored the movements of two together, weaving in and out amongst the prints of those who had walked this same path before them.

~

Barefooted and moving in sync along the intertidal lagoon, their hunt is not their own, and they know it. They slow at the sight of Wolf. The salt marshes and reed beds are shimmering in the sun, which makes them squint and burning rays of light bounce off the edge of Wolf's shiny tail, which is swished as though to shake it, them, off. Their Other has left paw prints in the mudflats, which have grown with the rise of a sultry summer, nutrient-rich now. Later, their respective hunter-gatherer dances will be revealed and then washed over by a new tide as though they never existed.

Woman and man are not scared of Wolf, but they want what Wolf wants. They too, follow the footprints of red deer, two larger impressions at the front of each print, and two smaller ones towards the back. They know what Wolf knows; if they find the legs that belong to these prints and catch them out, they will lead up to meat.

Wolf follows scent and intuition. Woman follows hunger and intuition. Both mothers think of the pack.

Mother Wolf is slim and lightly built, a herder, a darter, and a long-game player. Her young sometimes watch her amid the pack from the sidelines, stalking the stalker. The barefooted mother is on the left of the trail, the male in between their gaze, but she looks past and through him and his readied hunting tools and locks eyes with Mother Wolf. A return gaze shows she knows she is out of the game, for now. Slinks away toward her pack. Tail down, tip brushing sludgy sand. The herd of red deer are up ahead with some of their young calves. Bandy-legs trembling at the sound of the ground moving.

They were once safely hidden in this salty undergrowth as fawns. The mother prepares the carcasses, being careful not to get her fingers burnt. Cooks the meat. Her children play whilst they wait, dancing around the bodies of small red ones. A rivulet of dripping blood and their little feet moving in rhythm turns the sand and silt from gold to dark brown-red and leaves imprints around three-thirds the size of a razor fish shell.

~

The home looks out over the Irish Sea, past the men with iron fists, to the wind farm, turbines spin dizzyingly as though to mimic her confusion. Teacher had requested a room at the back for her. Colder. But warmer for when she is lifted to get dressed or have her body washed, and she can see a familiar stretch out of the window as she lifts her arms for the carers. Seagulls' squalls sound like the wrong radio channel or interference. She smiles through the glass window at a stranger. Her eyesight has faded, but not the colour of her eyes. They reflect the water in the near distance. Blue-grey and still. A humming, she is humming something. No, not a tune. Her body is reverberating every sound she has ever heard and every moment she has felt. And as she sings this story, it is a complicated song, and so her body moves in a way that looks as though something is trying to jump out from beneath her breast. But it gets stuck and tries to redirect itself, so her arm twitches frantically, trying to carry along its length a message. Fingertip hot. All of the limbs dance out of step, trying to emit what is steeped within her bones. Her crepey neck, though still elegant, is skyward with the sound.

Teacher hadn't wanted to send her away. Even now, with the seashell to his ear, the one they had kept and shown their small ones, though loud and instant, he can only hear old tides pulled by past moons. But she had fallen off the bed when he was cleaning up her messes. A vase smashed. Pretty duck egg blue with painted yellow flowers in pieces on the floor along with her teeth. And he had covered his eyes like he was driving around a bend on a country lane, and the sun had chosen to blind him just at the moment he had come across a field of too-yellow rapeseed. His reflexes are not what they used to be; he could not catch her fast enough.

He is walking now. He is waving. It is important to note that Teacher had taken up his remembering hobby long before she got this way. He walks a little further out along the shore towards the promenade, where the buildings start to line up like school children in the dinner line, hungry to steal the view. A faded green house has its back to him, first in the queue. Teacher looks up to see a ghost of a smile looking out and past him, and then there is nothing, just an empty window. He takes out his ruler and camera and points towards the vacant space in the air in the direction of the retraction of the ghost smile. *Snap.* Perhaps after the darkroom, something will be there, found in the reflection of the window. There is always more than the eye can see. His ruler, which he also holds up towards the fading light, fails to measure what can only be felt.

The carer bathes her gently. Slowly. They will not need to rush to get to her room again, tick her off on a list, or record this process in the future. The ink that writes her name on paper records will fade. The wind turbines stop like broken clocks, stand still for a few moments, and then change direction. Her hum travels through the open window out on the salt air breeze, and the wings of the turbines pick up her energy. They spin frenzied memories and peaceful ones too, into the air, which collide like red arrows amid a bird strike at an air show. Cormorants blow upside down in the sky as though executing a loop de loop.

Her humming becomes slower, and the sand falls through faster.

~

Sanderlings dance on the breeze. And skitter scatter here and there. They dance. The heat is stifling, and they move as though half-drunk to the last song in the DJ set. The shoreline is a dated function room with its wallpaper peeling and carpets all stained and sticky. Some waders' bodies become much smaller as they move because where they have flown from has been competing with the heat here, with extra snow there, and this meant fewer places to feed and nest.

This is a kids' disco. And all the young'uns are crying for treats, and the collective noise grows much louder until even the people far over the water hear the cries carried over by the wind, and they wonder.

Their first dance had been to Layla by Eric Clapton, not an obvious choice for a wedding song, but only the two of them knew that a new sort of love was coming. They would have married anyway. It wasn't like that. But they wanted to do things properly, not for their parents or anyone else, but for themselves, for each other. They grew and flew far from the nest at times, but always returned. Mixing up expected roles. It took so much to build that nest, so much intricate weaving.

A new tide is revealing. Teacher has something in a plaster cast now, not a limb of his own, broken or torn, but the shape left behind by another. Teacher didn't know it, but when he was gone too and buried with his wife, the plaster casts would be taken and presented in a museum. Dedicated to the people and love that came before his people and love, and the people and love that would come after. Children would walk across the floor and place their feet in those moments and imagine the ones the tide had taken too.

If someone had approached him on the beach on any day over the decades he spent there being curious, he could have spoken to them in Anglo-Saxon, *Ur byþ anmod ond oferhyrned, felafrecne deor, feohteþ mid hornum, mære mor-stapa; þæt is modig wuht.* Meaning the Auroch is bold and lofty-horned, a very savage beast it fights with its horns, a renowned strider across marshy terrain, it is a noble crea-ture. On his last day, just as he went to make a note of some markings, the crisscross of the crane birds engraved there long ago. He looked up and thought he saw one overhead flying towards him, with its long neck outstretched and full of grace, though they no longer flew this way.

# Sea Monster

There is a home in this small fishing village for those who have forgotten what their lives—Before the erosion of language and landscape, its place name translated into the peninsula of the whale or sea monster. The monster changed shape. A pebble trail of houses along the Wild Atlantic Way leaves clues as to the way that came before. One house as weary as its occupants juts into the jugular of the bay. A woman walks down the staircase, her face long frozen by the bitter Atlantic. A doorbell competes with the chime of the electronic church bells installed in St. Teresa's to mark the start of a mass no one will attend. A pale finger, not sea-weathered nor calloused from menial work, presses against the doorbell, which does not show its age due to a lack of touch. He had come to find out more about the baby who had floated up. As a clue to the timing of those terrible events.

A seafoam green door swings backwards as the white digit retrieves itself. The door is a gateway for those who have gone to the other side or started to submerge at least. A home for those who have been forgotten and vice versa.

One resident has been remembered now, though, for her expertise, but does she remember? It is worth a shot. *Nobody,* Frozen Face Lady tells the young Garda and a man in a dark suit. He looks as though salt from the sea mist rubbed part of his face away, but he hasn't been here long enough. Well, when they insisted on checking the records, there was a visit some twenty years earlier. Marked down for the same reason as theirs under reason for visit in the electronic visitor logbook. Nora hadn't said anything that time when quizzed, just looked right ahead. Frozen Face knew that as soon as she went to fetch the tea, they would be looking for other responses. *Did a blink or a certain clouding of her eyes mean yes or no?*

She is swimming deep underwater, free and lost amongst the island wrecks. At times in the land of awake, a certain gravitational pull of the sun, moon, and planets makes it so that the tide exposes bits of the past. A tip of a castle turret, a raggedy edge of fallen fell. To observers, her eyeballs look like unborns in utero rolling around rapidly through sealed skin, the world only a bodily opening away. She sees herself skipping by the cillín, dropping flowers for those her father said were unbaptized. Stones place marking souls. Nora counted them once, wondering whether the stone sizes would correlate to age if, one day, their little bodies were dug up or loosened from the earth by some natural disaster.

Violent movements accompany the dreams, which are one of the first signs. They might even come before the loss of memory. Some try to act out their nightmares, hitting or yelling in fear or both. Papery hands push forward and fan out against the imaginary swell of an ocean, aggressively circling to diminish the chances of sinking, drowning down there. She momentarily drops, sinks a foot or two. Arms propel up in alarm, trying to catch onto anything—kelp reefs, no, too slippery—a disused telecom pole. A green woollen blanket falls to the floor. Nora pushes forward, head bent down with direction, deeper to reach the treasures. Learning to breathe in new waters, to get back to before. Just once, she had dreamed of a soft, reassuring arm laid across her body, *Hush, hush, it is just a dream.* The voice of her mother from her infant days, that someone had cared enough to try to recreate. But there was never a soft arm, just a soft taut strap. Maybe that is how the man in the dark suit and the eroded face had got to her. A touch on her shoulder. *Are they looking after you? Feeding you well?* Just loud enough for Frozen Face Lady to overhear. Not a serious investigation, just something a relative or loved one might have said. He imagined a long-lost nephew sitting in his seat right now and placed the same wry, conspiratorial grin such a nephew may have had on his face at the end of each question.

Four exhibits lay in the middle of the table. They represented a wide range of biological materials that could be transferred during a crime. From blood to botanical materials, body fluids to textiles fibres, to hair. The examination of transferred botanical materials had not featured as a major consideration in forensic analysis until she came along. The shining star of the game in her heyday. They mixed the specimens up on the table in front of Nora, only to be met by a vacant stare. They reshuffled them like a magician mixing up cards, but with the opposite hope. There were hundreds of exhibits to get through, but they had to start small. Like with the coloured building blocks, age three up, the home activities coordinator used for the residents. Always starting with four blocks, working up to six, eight, and then ten. Build, deconstruct, rebuild. The body, or rather bones of the baby, had floated up above sea level.

Sealed in a rotten potato sack, they guessed it might have come from the cillín field. Where did that place the timing of events? Other corpses had come up before, from the sunken cemetery of St. Caomhan's Church, blessed bodies, and that place was sinking long before the islands. A row of Celtic Cross headstones from there had washed up, too, names and dates. Severed stones crossing borders, life from ending up in one place, life to, in another.

As a child, the woman looking blankly at the exhibits roamed the islands without care, clearing whole hedgerows of pollutant-free blackberries. People wondered why she had developed the condition so early when she had grown up with the purest air there was that side of the Atlantic. Though she had set her sights on further away, outside of herself, away from the smallest bubble before it could burst. Head down again, an ache in the neck and upper shoulders that never goes away. Her body's memory of decades spent looking down a microscope. There was one case that never left her, and sometimes she returns to it as if, in this new dream world, she could finally solve the unsolved. A sub-sample—pollen grain—she had been looking for a certain shape, size, and a match to match the crime. Those poor children.

The green woollen blanket comforts her body as it shakes through the effort of her eyes scanning an imagined grain, up and down, neck moving in sync with the machine as though she were it. Images are stacked together like a pack of cards and transformed into a three-dimensional image of the pollen grain. The strangest thing was that there hadn't been a mark on them. She had collected samples from the field, knelt as though in prayer, snowdrops sang a final hymn, swaying by their sweet little heads. Nora lay back now, just like them, still and silent with the sky above them and her through the skylight of the home, its blue hues an eternal silent witness.

The thing with living in the mouth of something is that it can swallow you whole if you're not careful. That had been the problem for the islands; they had been right in the mouth of Galway Bay. Some of the islanders had tried to take matters into their own hands to become more self-sufficient and sustainable. Community-owned wind power, retrofit homes, and a move away from dependence on fossil fuels for transport. She had been going to return home and retire in one of those retrofit homes. A nice little garden full of wildflowers and a couple of sheep for grazing. A retro yellow kettle that whistled and a radio for company. But the monster took her around the same time it took the islands. She felt like she had been presented with two paths in life, and she had struggled to know which one to take. The two main roads of the islands running parallel from east to west had been attacked by something on the day she had left— three big bites were taken out of them in different places, and the lower road at sea level could not run fast enough. It had never happened before, not like that.

The man in the suit is sitting so close to her that the frayed edges of the green woollen blanket are almost touching his knees. *Biscuit?* He holds out his hand with a perfect circle in his upturned palm and looks up at her. Head bent back as though on the other side again now, but she looks back down at the sound of his voice and takes it from him and then throws it over her shoulder towards the fireplace as if disposing of evidence. The biscuit breaks into uneven cracks, crumbling into dust. They return to the items on the table. These items could be used to identify what happened. *Where did they end up?* He asks her, *Have they been moved, perhaps?* He needs her help. Salt Mist Face doesn't know how to work out the unique signatures of each suspected environment. He knows when the earth is moved by a spade or even a machine built for such a dark task, certain plants will quickly invade the fresh surface, other species will follow in succession until the area recovers. He is trying to work out a timeframe for when everything sank. *Nora*, he says, *Ecology is much like humanity but more truthful in its evolution, huh?* He reshuffles the exhibits again. Her eyes roll and seem to hover over the fourth to his right. A small soil sample in a sealed packet, almost rust-red.

*Where did you find him?* she asks. *Who?* Says the man in black. *You know,* she says, *I left them flowers.*

*Fun time*, the activities coordinator calls out. This week, it's animal therapy. There was a small Irish pony from Connemara in the home vegetable garden, trying to steal the food. Specially trained to deal with people like the residents and personally selected by its trainer for its laid-back personality. The green woollen blanket covers her knees over her overcoat outside in the cold air. Her chair is pushed up the steep incline around the back of the home, its veranda built higher now than predicted sea level, but sometimes it is level. The Irish pony nudges its head gently in her hands, and she cries out, not something she does often. She is back in a faraway farm field, the outback, and the foul sweet smell of incinerated horse meat and Boronia flowers melted into a syrup. Amongst the bodies, she had found the burnt-out carcasses of a mare and foal, limbs entangled, foal still suckling as though its mother's milk could save it.

For his last visit, the man in the dark suit decides to come at peak sundowning. To try and take advantage of her dreams and fears, to watch them being played out, to try to get inside them. This will be down to luck and experiment, he acknowledges. He just wants to give them dignity, to give her dignity, to give the nameless names, to give a death a cause, to give a cause for death, to give a body, all bodies, a final resting place.

To save a whole load of people from passing through history lost in time, swimming in ambiguous grief. Covered and covered up. He waits for the fragile hands to stop swimming so he knows she has come back. As the hands come down to her lap after one last circling motion, he edges closer to the flowery settee she is sitting upon. He places the machine right under her nose with mysteries on the slide as if trying to direct where her dreams may go next. He grasps her hand gently as it makes to go upwards again. She flinches at the touch, unused to physical contact, and he worries she will shout out, but her face softens.

Underneath her lids, the rolling becomes less rapid. He guides Nora's hand over the machine, and she feels it in her sleep, as though blind but with all of her other senses about her. There are only two samples to choose from if she just opens her eyes and looks, as with the two paths in life she was presented with a long time ago, and she had been unclear on which one to take then too. He still has hope. *Blank.* She can't tell him; it is already lost.

# FOSSIL FLOWER MAN

For Deryn Rees-Jones

*The flowers of life are but visionary. How many pass away and leave no trace behind!*
—Johann Wolfgang Goethe, *The Sorrows of Werter,* 1774

In the future, when the remaining foundations of Oxford's Ashmolean Museum were exhumed, archaeologists found the fossilised remains of the 17th-century Welsh botanist Edward Lhuyd, and within the fossil of him, they found the fossilised flowers of the Snowdon Lily. Or Lloydia serotina, the name he had given to them as an eternal reminder of himself. Alas, they were renamed but not forgotten. They had fossilised, or rather charcoalified, with him in his old jacket pocket. Long after he was gone and long after they had gone too, they continued to live together through the preservation of memory. Men like Lhuyd and the fossil flowers were and still are quite rare. Hundreds of millions of years ago, the world's first fossil flowers had burned bright in wildfires—ancient angiosperms—and then hid in the dark.

When wildfire phenomena last occurred towards the end of the late Jurassic and through parts of the Cretaceous period, it was during the dinosaurs' last days. Lhuyd's fossilised charcoalified body lies on a lab table, and alongside him is a slide with the fossilised charcoalified Snowdon Lily. A youngish woman, an emerging forensic ecologist with a lot to prove, is examining him and examining the flowers. She takes a sip of her elderflower tea, and some of it splashes onto her white lab coat as she jerks suddenly, having noticed a peculiar expression on Lhuyd's face. He had been buried in the Welsh Aisle of St. Michael's Church, Oxford, after being found dead in his room in the Ashmolean Museum in 1709 at the age of 49. Records indicated he had died of pleurisy after becoming vulnerable to respiratory infections since he developed asthma during his pioneering botanist field trips across all the counties of Wales. And it was whilst he was in North Wales, where he came across the then not-even-in-flower Snowdon Lily in 1698, and he christened it, and he knew it was something special just by looking at its grass-like leaves, that his chest began to tighten.

He didn't need to see it in bloom to know it was special. Had he only known what fate lay in store for the Snowdon Lily, or as the Welsh liked to call it, *brwynddail y mynydd*, meaning rush-leaves of the mountain. That this rare plant—

an ice age relic—would become the first flora in Great Britain and Wales to become extinct due to human-caused climate change.

The world warmed, and this Arctic-alpine flora's ideal alpine conditions for survival were no longer viable, and so the Snowdon Lily perished. The mountain *Yr Wyddfa* and its pathways began to soften, and walkers slipped more and more, and people stopped going up as much because seeing the sunrise or set on its summit wasn't worth dying for, all for a photo. In general, historically, walkers didn't see the Snowdon Lily; it was safely tucked away at the highest point of the rocks on inaccessible ledges. This flora preferred north or northeast-facing crags, unreachable by those without specialist skills and knowledge.

In the Victorian era, plant hunters came and climbed—when the flowers were more in abundance—and the hunters could be seen swinging off a rock with one hand whilst stuffing their caps with delicate yellows and whites. Colonising. Then hungry sheep had come for them and grazed and grazed, and that was their first major undoing, but the melting of the ice and snow and its refusal to form again was what made them lose their final footing. Lhuyd had been an illegitimate child; his parents, unusually for the times, were unmarried, and so he made it his life's work to give christened names to things. He took control of naming and language, reclaiming wherever he could: the Cornish dialect and dinosaur fish. Claiming the Celtic roots of his own name as an adult, he demanded to be referred to as Lhuyd and not his given name of Lloyd. When Lhuyd died, he was in debt to the university, which never paid him a farthing for his museum-keeping duties, but they came and collected the debts he owed them in the form of all of his life's works before the last rites had even been finished.

The young woman in the forensic lab listens to the radio as she works, and Lou Reed's *Perfect Day* comes on; Reed's disembodied voice is singing, *Just a perfect day / Drink sangria in a park … / Just a perfect day / You make me forget myself*. In her head, she mishears – but hears the words in the exact same tune – *Just a perfect day / Wildfires in the park / … / And then later when it gets dark / We'll go home*, she feels somebody watching her at the door as she sings along taking notes of the specimens, and she looks up. No one is there. Lhuyd was a man of firsts, but this kind of a first was a puzzle to all in her field. Usually, bodies burn when they come into contact with fire, and his body had been buried for hundreds of years, so it should have naturally skeletonised and turned to dust by now, if anything. But here he was, intact and preserved, though slightly charcoal-y.

There was also the fact that his body was found under the museum and not in the recorded burial place in the church grounds. Maybe in the afterlife, his spirit was disturbed as he remembered he had forgotten to add some notes or classifications to his body of work. So, his ghost had risen and made its way back to the museum to make his final amendments, and once there, he had been caught up in the Big Fire.

There had been no need to exhume his body before now. One hypothesis was that the stone foundations around him had created a vacuum, and combined with limited oxygen and nearby burning tree roots, it led to the smoke and charcoalification of his body and the flowers. But just how had he and they stayed intact til this moment? It was a miracle. According to nature, according to science, at least. He had been a man who had ensured that the memories of so many lives across multi-species had lived on in his finding and naming of them, but those in positions of power had sought to quickly forget him and show off his found treasure as their own. And now he had been dug up in almost immaculate condition, and so his eccentric achievements had been resurrected.

History books showed that Oxfordshire firefighters had tackled nearly 250 wildfires at the peak of the heatwave in the summer of 2022. By the time the fire came that put out all of history, well, the history in the Ashmolean – ancient sun discs, camel tombs, and coins of emperors – wildfires were in the 1000s each heatwave season, and heatwaves were no longer restricted to a season. The grasslands, woodlands, and crops of Oxfordshire had smoked like an old man falling asleep in a comfortable armchair, drunk on a nightcap of whisky and oblivious to the flickering flames at his feet, an undocked cigar having caught at the worn fringes of his blanket comforter, he had been celebrating selling off his land, and unwittingly set himself alight. He had packed his bags for somewhere more temperate and wasn't looking back. The last in the line of a dwindling aristocracy, and now that aristocracy was extinct. Local councillors had cried over such an estate being placed into corporate hands, and the specialist estate agent had advertised it as, *The single most significant ring-fenced carbon offsetting opportunity to come to the open market in England.* The fire had spread from the countryside and into the city, along the rivers, past the wickered AI bikes, until it reached the Oxford campus and the Ashmolean Museum.

Ironically, one of the first things to catch fire was the artwork "A Forest Fire' by Piero di Cosimo (1462–1522), oil on panel, and so the flames ignited eagerly and spat their embers onto the past, as depicted within di Cosimo's frame. And the curator's notes, *The power and beauty of nature are depicted in this extensive landscape as the terrifying spectacle of a burning forest creates fear and panic among birds, animals and human beings,* were licked and lost.

Two model, highly fund-worthy doctoral students working on the cure for carbon capture ran screaming from the Bodleian library buildings, quantitative data in hand. They had been part of a group trying to save the ancient manuscripts as the fire reached the library buildings. They had been running carrying the *Codex Mendoza*, Aztec pictograms, side by side with their data on updating the UK government's plans to trap and store carbon under the North Sea. But sadly, their research perished with their bodies, and it was too late to share. Their bodies did not fossilise like Lhuyd and his Lloydia serotina, not even as trace fossils, and so all the memories were gone. High up or abstractly, even, in *The Cloud*—their information on carbon capture had been heavily protected with passwords only the two researchers knew and had sworn their lives on—academic research on carbon capture had become a target for corrupt corporations, carbon capture equalled currency, equalled power.

As the manor house of the last English aristocrat burned, so did all his books, and one, in particular, fell to the floor, a very valuable and rare set of botanical records by an eminent 17th-century Welsh botanist. The aristocrat had never really bothered to read the book; it had been passed down the family lineage for centuries, but he loved to show it off at dinner parties for anyone interested in nature. And as all the other books burned, this one didn't fully catch, like it had some strange holy seal around it, instead it lay on the ground curiously unaffected as the last ashes of *How to Keep an Aristocratic Title*'s pages burned and its last ashes landed on an open page of the miraculously preserved rare botanical book next to it, smudging though not ruining the description of *Lloydia serotina.*

The young woman in the white lab coat concentrates now, examining the Snowdon Lilies that were found in Lhuyd's coat pocket, the beauty of the micro- and macroscopic pieces of their leaves and shoots under her electronic microscope. She looks at the charcoalified button on his doublet and thinks how elegant he looks in his smoky sleep. She knows she shouldn't, especially ungloved, but she just wants to touch him, to feel him, this man whose physical being had survived the Big Fire, who had demonstrated so much perseverance despite having been apparently unloved. She imagines the Deans scurrying off into the night with his books and manuscripts as he lay taking his last breaths, and then toasting a drink to themselves after in the local pub, or a brothel house cum bar, or whatever. He had left no will and never been married, an Oxford dropout in his youth despite his continued life and death connection to there.

She wonders if he ever danced with a woman, and just in case he never had the chance, she starts to dance. She moves her body around his still body in motion with the music on the radio, and Reed's song is just finishing: /I thought I was someone else / Someone good. She puts her arm out to him, asking him to join her on the dance lab floor, and to her surprise, he rises. The music changes. Something a bit more upbeat. Faster. He is looking at her, mesmerised. Charcoal soot falls from his lashes; his eyes have been closed for a long time, and he has to blink them fully open. His joints are stiff, and he is wobbly on his feet as he first makes to get up off the examination table. The music has jumped back to the year of his death, and Bach's Prelude & Fugue in A Minor fills the room. She decides it is more lively than Reed but has a strange, eclectic "funeral" air to it, but still, she moves to it in an odd, jerky fashion. Their dance is a mix of improvised noughties dance club moves and Baroque, he leans and holds his arm out to her elegantly and tilts his chin towards her rather attractively, and she mirrors him with her own body, pulling the side of her white lab coat out to the hilt as though it is a fine dress of many ruffles and she mocks bows all the while maintaining eye contact. Then all of a sudden, he courtesies and, from his pocket, produces a flower twisted into a ring; it is the Snowdon Lily, and he has saved it.

# Sparkle Spitter

Once a stray cat of boats, now Queen of ancient wood. Plague by name, plague by nature. Infectious wonderer, giver of wonder. A cat of unknown origin, once placeless, nameless. *Paw, paw,* left, right. She plays *pat-a-cake* with a small mouse in between her front legs. It is still half alive. Using its last light within, the mouse scurries towards a giant oak: life-breath giver, extender. Tall, its leaves soon to drop. Mousey carries along with them the parts of their body that are already dead. Heavy, yet making light. To her dismay, Plague sees the mouse disappear by the base of the oak trunk, where gnarly twisted roots meet the earth. Mousey has disappeared into an invisible abyss.

Queen Plague had wanted to devour the creature's last shine and spit its sparkle back out as a gift.

She can no longer see Mousey. With her head tilted to the ground, she can just about make out a faint squeak from far down below or maybe in another lifetime. They say cats have nine lives, but what they mean is that they have nine chances to avoid the end. On closer inspection, Plague sees that Mousey has fallen into a deep time well and decides to follow.

*Jump. Down. Falling,* front paws out. Soft, peaty landing. Mustering all the spring within her feet, body... then *up again. Out.* Through another time door within the oak roots. One from before; at the start.

The woods have changed in name from Whirligig Wood to School Wood; the sign is gone, and her Mom's horse trailer, too. There is a horse and a cart in its place, and a young couple are walking nearby through a small pocket of the woods. It is like the woods Plague knows, but more thickset. They are passing through a canopy of hazel and elder now, and the sunlight spins through the trees, narrowing to form a hazy halo around the heads of the humans. An animal kicking flies away has noticed Plague and gives her a look. She cocks her ears and asks if the couple belong to him? He swishes his tail, *yes.*

The girl human is wearing a long white dress, flowing, though tightly gathered at the waist, as though to imprison her within herself. Ivy strangling. She carries a small booklet of something she looks at and then makes soft sounds out of, all coming from her pink rose lips. The boy human, and the birds of the woods prick their ears up and trail behind her at a respectable distance as she moves, moss, velvet underfoot.

Plague follows her because she still wants to find Mousey to devour its last shine and then spit the sparkle out as a gift for her Mom. She is not sure if the mouse will still be alive, though, and it would be better if Mousey were still beating because ebbing lights hold the most magic. And Plague had *pat-a-caked* it good. The human girl walks towards the water.

There is a small stream that looks familiar but fuller, almost swollen, like the belly of her other Mom, and Plague had been left out on the bankside then, too, alone, uninvited. But what was this? The girl human was beckoning her over, *ch, ch,* with her fingers. Plague approached, looking left, right, sniffing for danger. And then she saw it, right where the fingers were pointing. A gentle pulse left, just one *lub dub* to go—and then there was an inhalation which left Plague glowing, proud, full of shine.

But how will she get back home?


The white dress is twirling, spinning in circles. Mousey's body, lying next to the motion, will be still forever. It is making Plague feel dizzy. The hem is full of green now and dirt. The human is casting a spell for Plague, for her own self, too. Arms are flailing; it is all so fast; as she falls to the ground, the human girl emits three sounds which Plague is bound to keep. Safe forever.

And then Plague is *up*. Back. Stretching the last fibres of the oak tree's roots apart with her nose as she surfaces.

She sees two feet she knows and loves and spits the sparkle out.

# Super rat

The story you are about to read is one of a city rat's quest to survive ten years post Capital of Culture in Liverpool, UK, through being terrorised by the city council who want to cut him out whilst trying to stay true to his art criticism, avoid run-ins with the chief city pest controller and avenge the death of his father on the tenth anniversary of his passing. All during the 2018 Liverpool Biennial and Biennial Fringe. C is for culture, or more precisely, the CAPITAL of Culture.

§

Let me introduce myself. My name is Remington AS1220, or please, Rem for short. I was born in the year 2008, and I'm what Liverpool City Council's chief pest controller and long-time arch-enemy of mine, Derek McVey, would call a brown rat (Rattus norvegicus).

Also known as the common rat, street rat, sewer rat, Hanover rat, Norway rat, Norwegian rat, Parisian rat, water rat, or wharf rat. I was born in a back alley in Bootle, one frosty

New Year's Day. The first festive season on the cusp of the credit crunch, and Jesus thought he had it bad being born in a stable in Bethlehem. At least people could afford to bring him gifts, I mean, gold, for goodness sake! My parents had nothing to give me. Nothing. I was born at that slump point on New Year's Day when people hadn't even gotten up to put the bins out yet, so there were no scrumptious leftovers available.

My old man (may he rest in peace) broke into a two-up two-down terrace, and this was where he met his terrible fate. Out of desperation, he started chewing on the wire cable of a Remington AS1220 Amaze Smooth and Volume Air Styler, new out that year. Some Scouse bird was not impressed and called up the city council, kicking Raaaa off, and then they extinguished him. Poison. *I'm sorry.* I still find it hard to talk about. Anyway, that's where I got my name from. My mother named me after the one thing that caught my father out. As did I. Then she left me. Couldn't cope. It's OK. Don't feel sorry for me. Dry your eyes. I took on a new life; you see, New Year's Day in Liverpool in 2008 was no ordinary New Year's Day. It was, in fact, the beginning of Liverpool's year as the *Capital of Culture.*

So, I left my native Bootle backstreet and made my way to the big city. I had always fancied myself as a bit of an art critic, one with an eye for the aesthetic. The city's bumper visitor numbers and a multimillion-pound boost to its economy also meant more leftovers. My absolute favourite dish is leftover chips from outside the *Lobby*—you must fight the seagulls for them, mind. I've nearly lost an eye on a couple of occasions. My advantage is that I can crawl low to the ground and lie in wait for the Saturday night partygoers to stumble and drop a few—and if anyone spots me, they stop and scream: *A rat!* People are terrified of rats; we get a bad rep, but it means no one fights us for chips. *Here, take them*, said one gent from Newcastle. Whenever this happens, I'm always made up. *Made Up* was the theme of the Liverpool Biennial in 2008, and I, just a whipper snapper fresh to the city streets, was made up with all that was on offer. Super chuffed, in fact. It's said that rats can't see more than a few feet in front of them, but I know good art when I see it.

A decade later, this year's theme for the Biennial, and one adopted by others on the fringe circuit, is *Beautiful World, Where Are You? Beautiful World, Where Are You?* indeed. You see, right now, my world isn't looking so beautiful. I've been made homeless. That's right. I had a home. I had digs in a building on Hanover Street (rather apt for a Hanover rat), a place that housed artists, designers, and independent creatives. One of the last affordable commercial premises in town—sure, it got drafty and needed some TLC—but there was no need to sell it from under our feet (or claws). You guessed it. Developers. Developers are the *un-developers* of the art world. They take affordable spaces, and sometimes they don't even finish what they've taken. An artist *always* finishes a job. Even if they run out of money, they *believe* in their work.

We were given notice, of course, but it was sad. An end of an era. Ten years of living in the basement of a creative hub, and I would have to find somewhere new. Start all over again. I decided to cheer myself up by going to check out some exhibitions. You may wonder how and where I communicate my reviews. Fridays at 2 am, at the side steps of the Bombed Out Church.

Atmospheric. I don't get a massive crowd, but I keep them coming back. You see, I bring them the good stuff, the independent stuff.

I decided to set off to the old George Henry Lees building to see a piece of work that I believe was inspired by me. The *Super Rat* sculpture. You may think it narcissistic of me to assume so, and no, I haven't had it confirmed by the artist themself, but I see myself in it. I crept up to the window one fine day on my hind legs, and there it was in all its enormous glory. A sublime structure of polymer clay with shining pink eyes and an effervescent white coat. I was moved. Emotionally. Good art does that. Yes, I'm just a small brown rat. Yet, *Super Rat* epitomises everything a rat stands for. Our daily struggles. Our tenaciousness. Our will to live. *Super Rat* stands tall and says, *I'm not going anywhere; I matter. I stand with you and all of you.* The paper pushers keep trying to cut us out. No space for the smaller creatures. I've dodged five bags of poison in the last 48 hours alone. I know who is placing them there—my oldest enemy, chief city pest controller Derek McVey. The same man who killed my father all those years ago. To him, there's no room for our kind; he sees us as taking from them. Using up resources meant for those higher up the food chain. Yet, we have a right to be seen and heard. I came face to face with him the other week in a shop on Bold St. *You killed my father, prepare to die!* I hissed. Yes, I'm a film critic too. He just looked at me in disgust and put more poison down. He knows my pointy face by now. *That should be enough to take the whole street out,* he said with an evil laugh.

I'm the only one he hasn't been able to kill during his whole career. Sometimes I run off, hoping he'll chase me into the path of an oncoming car. Or trip and fall down the stairs. I bait him. Hiss at him. Do all I can to goad him. I took one last look in the window at *Super Rat*, and I felt emboldened, renewed. *Super Rat* fixed his gaze on me—transferring his power to me—I am now invincible. They can't cut me out. I jot down a few mental notes for my next review evening at the 'Bomby' and move on. In the dead of night, I sneak into St. Johns Market. There's an exhibition on as part of the Biennial fringe, and my hunger for art is stronger than my hunger for chips right now. Whenever I'm troubled, I go to art. Art is my therapy. I listen carefully for footsteps, nothing.

We rats don't necessarily have better hearing than humans, but we can hear at a higher frequency. If the alarm goes off, I'll hear it before the security. Something catches my eye. Big pictures are all blown up in aerial view. It's like my world from down below but from up above. I am lost in them. I climb up a nearby chair to look closer; the artwork label says Humanscape. I mull the words over in my head: human and scape. I want to scape from the humans—well, the ones in power who won't let me live my life. I wonder if I might be on one of these blown-up photographic beauties that represent all of the injustices of our society. *Am I there?*

*Am I a speck on the horizon?* I'm about to move closer to see if I can spot myself when I hear it. *Beep. Beep. Beep.* It's the alarm. Footsteps. The security man is coming towards me—I fall down off the chair—I'm more below the world that looks down on me now than ever before. I flip up off my back, taking one last look at the photos and flee. I know security will call pest control. Derek McVey will be back. I'll be waiting for him.

Tired after a full day of taking in all the fabulous art on the fringe circuit, I scuttle back to my Hanover Street quarters whilst I can. I get back, and when I try to slip through my usual air brick, I find it has been boarded up with a *building work in progress* sign over it. This really isn't my day. I start running, running as fast as possible. I run back to the old George Henry Lees building to find *Super Rat*. I need a pep talk. But then I look in the window and see something else. A multitude of colours, black zig-zags, pinks and reds, and yellows too. I am transfixed. The swirls match my emotions. I read the name, A Long the Riverrun. I run and run and run.

They say rats normally only live for two years or so, and I'd been going for ten. When you have a lifelong grudge, it keeps you going. I knew the day I avenged my father would be the day I could finally close my weary eyes and die in peace. This was how it happened. It was towards the end of the art festival, and I'd given a review at the 'Bomby' one night to resounding applause. I decided to treat myself to an up-close viewing of *Super Rat* before it was moved on (as all rats eventually are). I had crept into the old George Henry Lees building to get my whiskers as close as possible. Then it happened. A trap. I must have jumped up ten feet in the air and startled Derek McVey, who was lying in wait. He fell back against *Super Rat*, whose form had started to tilt towards my old enemy as if in slow motion, falling forward. A giant shuddering shook the window display. A pale hand stuck out from underneath a mass of polymer clay… *Super Rat's* eyes held a victorious glint, and McVey's hand twitched a few times… I hissed, *You killed my father, prepare to die—twitch—* and then he was gone. *Super Rat* and I exchanged a look, and, laying my bloody head against his shoulder, I closed my eyes. For the last time.

# TWITCHERS' TROPICANA

The brown beard starts twitching as it scrolls through the news on a handheld device. *Twitch. Twitch. Twitch.* The twitching movements become more agitated as the owner of said beard scrolls further, delving deeper into the news feeds, clicking links that take them into more links on a screen with the illuminated image of a bluebird in the right-hand corner. The bird which never seems to leave or migrate, and then the chin the beard rests upon looks as though it will take off itself, do the bluebird's job for it. If *only* they had a mini-sub or a Gulfstream G700, or a Tesla. The twitching movements carry them forward to the shoe rack. It is a hot day, and they might have considered wearing sandals if they could think logically through the twitching. *Twitch. Twitch. Twitch.* The movements run through them and force them almost all the way through the door without stopping, but the brown beard uses all their force to turn, just for a split second, and grab the nearest footwear to hand off the rack. Thick hiking boots coloured brown with the excrement of earth. The boots are twitching all the way on the connecting buses, *tappety-tap, twitch, tappety-tap, twitch,* to the small Cornish coastal town where the sightings were reported, and with each stop, each ring of the bell, the brown beard convulses in consternation, checking their watch, with each *brrnnngg,* comes an ever-twitchier *twitch, twitch, twitch.*

The brown booby starts its descent into stillness. It has flown from the Tropics far, far out into this Cornish bay and stands on a rock, perched there with its yellow webbed feet holding it in place serenely, casually observing its prey just under the surface of the water. A crowd of twitching faces watches the brown booby, *twitch, twitch, twitch,* all eyes and furry eyebrows twisting towards the creature. Their facial muscles are refashioned and frenzied into a new bodily memory in the direction of this rare tropical bird. Each twitcher is lined up against the sea wall; all are in a long row, with big cameras and long lenses sticking out towards the bird. They look like an anxious army, *twitch, twitch, twitch,* with their Canons loaded and ready to fire.

The brown booby is usually seen around the Caribbean, Mexico, Colombia, and Venezuela. The nearest it usually gets to their shores is Spain. Warming weather had created this opportunity for the Twitchers, an event that 'in the know' birders refer to as the *Twitchers' Tropicana.* The brown booby is rare in that it has no brood patch to warm its eggs during incubation; instead, it stands on its eggs. Their highly vascularized webbed feet act as heating pads that transfer brown booby body heat to their developing eggs, which also protects the eggs from the scorching sun, from becoming fried, sunny side up.

This bird is relaxing, but at the same time, still thinking about going in for the fish, skim-plunge style, and as it appears to be about to shift, the sounds of the firing 'clicks' squad go into overdrive and lenses lengthen in anticipation of the brown booby's next movements, *click, click, click.*

And then, *Twitch,* it is gone, as though it was never there.

The brown beard twitches on the connecting buses all the way back home, but now their *twitches* are like the batteries running out on a kid's wind-up toy from three Christmases ago. They press play on the camera and zoom in on the face of the brown booby, noting the dark brown hood and the peculiar way it falls over its body, leaving an exposed and unsettling white face, like a cloak over the body of a messenger of death. Brown beard decides that the brown booby looks just like a cartoon image of the Grim Reaper, but they can't bring themselves to delete what still makes them *twitch, twitch, twitch.*

# Turkey neck

*This is life's ultimate cruelty. It offers us a taste of youth and vitality, and then it makes us witness our own decay.*
—Isabella Rossellini, *Death Becomes Her* (1992)

*How to cure turkey neck?* A woman with a neck of self-perceived concern types these words into an internet search engine. First of all, she examines the corresponding images that come up to see if, yes, this really is her problem. A real-life turkey turns up, lost amongst the images of *before and after* women on plastic surgery and cosmetic companies' websites. Its droopy neck stands out from the other *turkey necks*; this turkey neck is bright red, jubilant, and unashamed. Its beady bird eye looks the internet searcher right in the eye as if to say, *I know why you're here.*

She has to admit, she doesn't usually think of them like that, so bold and beautiful and proud. The woman usually thinks of them at Christmas as bland and white pieces of meat around the dinner table camouflaged by gravy and, eventually, someone's Boxing Day leftovers. What happens to the turkey's red fancy frill on its neck once it is dead, she wonders? Its frill, or caruncle, is the colour of Christmas, of baubles and decorations and bows upon gifts for loved ones. But once dead, the stain left behind is of dirty snow, of unbecoming, of melting away from life, and the next day, well after Boxing Day, as with the snow, it is like it never existed.

She decides she would like to buy a turkey killed in its entire state, whole being, and take off its red frilly neck and place it in a box at Christmas time with the other red bows as a memory, and take it out each year and place it somewhere as a reminder of something, perhaps of memories and what it takes to have them and make them, and of how you can't avoid them. Especially when there are red frills and bows about, and your life's past is inescapable, with every Christmas song, it is in the window of your mind's eyes – your past – is in an indestructible snow globe with glitter, even if it was not all that glittery. This is what red frills mean to her, and by visual association, the turkey's neck, too.

The internet tells her that each Christmas, 100,000,000 turkeys are killed; well, *that's 100,000,000 wishes*, she thinks. She reads that the turkey's wishbone is a forked bone that supports the bird's chest when in flight. Their wishbone, once the turkey is dead and cooked, is pulled apart by human beings, and the person left with the bigger part is the winner or said to have their wish granted; if both parts are equal in size, both people get their wish. The woman wonders if a turkey could get one wish, solo or shared; what would that be?

She turns her thoughts back to the problem at hand, her own potential *turkey neck*. The woman tries to imagine if ageing turkeys had access to the internet, and were to type in *forty-plus female human necks*, would they feel it was a fair comparison? If they had the chance to examine this anthropomorphism of their beautiful bill. The internet is sad to tell her that at around the age of forty, many women start to notice a decline in the appearance of their necks. After all its decades of hard work, holding their heads up high, well as high as possible. Sometimes their heads had drooped during times of tiredness or sadness, or relaxation for those women who had reached forty and regularly experienced such a thing.

And you see, some women had willingly let the muscles in their neck fold into worries like tension origami, and the damage was done.

Random facts jump out at her from the page, and she leans forward; as she does so, her neck leans forward with her. Conscious of this and what has led her to this search for answers, she tries to hold her neck back a little, like a wild fowl bird breaking loose from a pen; she holds its muscles on either side taut, as if holding a bird by its wings to secure it. She reads the facts: *the underlying platysma muscles start to detach and loosen, and their edges show through the skin as vertical bands from the chin to the collarbone.* The internet is harsh: it tells her *you can choose to accept this or hide it with turtlenecks*—make like a turtle and draw your neck in and out of your shell—or *you could visit a medical professional for effective treatment.*

Like the slinkys she used to throw down the stairs as a kid, this new neck with its loose bands is a reminder of the youth she once had, *and what you see is turkey neck.* She is not sure she likes this news; she will eat collagen supplements for breakfast! She knows she won't, that she will forget, like the postnatal exercises and drinking two litres of water a day, but she'll still be bothered every time her turkey neck ruins a perfectly good photo, every time it reminds her.

She steps into the bathroom, into the mirror, and slowly peels away the shoulders of her top, exposing her collarbone, and her upper breastbone; her neck is still not quite in the frame, though. *Aha,* she sees a bobble on the side, it's a miracle. She ties her hair up off her face, and then it's there, exposed, her neck in the dead centre of the frame of the mirror. The woman steps back a little, like she is at the Louvre, viewing the Mona Lisa, and she needs to be not too close nor too far away, to appreciate the art. She thinks about Mona Lisa's neck for a second; it is quite short, stubby, no? She shakes herself; no, she must concentrate on judging herself right now, not the Mona Lisa! The woman is ready again now. She looks in the mirror and shifts her head to the left, then to the right, slightly arching her head back to expose the sinews of her neck as she imagines a professional dancer might do.

The problem is, compared to many of her friends in their forties, too, her neck is long; there is more of it to turn *turkey*. One bit of advice from the internet says to try facial yoga, *close your mouth while puckering your lips as if you are trying to kiss the ceiling or lower your head, but with control, to increase the flow of blood to the area.* The woman had read that when a turkey is killed, it is hung upside down and shackled by its legs, stunned, and has its throat slit on a circular blade. She rotates her neck in the mirror in a clockwise circular motion, as advised by a YouTube anti-ageing yoga guru, then in an anti-clockwise direction, for three repetitions each way.

The air is sharp against her neck from a breeze through the open bathroom window, and she imagines she is a turkey hanging upside down on the line, and the wind is a blade preparing her for the boiling, for the de-feathering, for the losing of her beauty, the removal of her red frill. She takes an anti-ageing oil and rubs it into her neck—all while maintaining eye contact with herself—she sees in the mirror another image, the rosehip oil, with its pink tint, becomes the blood of the turkey, and it's pouring down her neck, *pouring, pouring, pouring*, until she has used the whole bottle before she knows it, and the turkey is looking back at her, bled out.

She has a flashback to a scene from one of her favourite movies from the nineties, in which Goldie and Meryl take a potion to cheat the ageing process and, in turn, end up fooling themselves. She particularly likes a bit where Meryl is facing the mirror, just as she is now, and Meryl has just taken a magic potion to return her youth, and in her mirror, Meryl gasps with delight as her own neck tightens and lifts and shrinks back into another lifetime, *I'm a girlll*, Meryl says, with stars in her eyes. But, girls, as the woman has come to realise, are not so wise.

# THE COST OF LIVING

*After Lydia Davis*

She is standing there staring at the eggs on the supermarket shelf. She's trying to break it down.

In her head, she does the maths:

Each frozen embryo transfer cost her about £2000. And then Jill fucking left when they never hatched. £8800 for a multi-cycle package with fertility care. 6 blastocysts. Good value, really, if it had worked. The last time she checked Jill's Insta—every hour since she had fucked off—Jill was lying on a hotel bed in Berlin, having just got back in from a night out with a young blonde thing tucked under her armpit, like a chick she was trying to keep warm and incubate without breaking.

Jill was good at breaking things. She had liked that about her at the time. Found her clumsiness endearing. And now she was fucking broken and trying to do the maths with her head wrecked and literally broke. She considers her options:

10 purely organic eggs—mixed weight—£4.50 a box, so that equals 45p per egg. She'd read an article when she was trying, about how organic eggs have much higher omega-3 fatty acids than the low-quality ones, and that omega-3 fatty

acids were really important when you were trying because they help to regulate a woman's hormones—essential for ovulation—and increasing blood flow to the uterus. Next up, 12 medium free-range eggs, £3.10 a box. The average human female needs around 45g of protein per day, and each individual egg, no matter its quality, is said to have approximately 13g of protein each. So, at 25.8p each for the box of 12 medium free-range eggs, over a week in the life of an average female human, that's going on 2/3 of the way to meeting a woman's daily requirements.

The essentials range on the lower shelf has a box with 15 eggs for £1.99, so just 13.3p an egg. She considers the hens and all the eggs they never got to see hatched. She visualises them in battery cages; all lined up and with their heads straining through the bars to feed, causing a de-feathering on their necks and heads where the bars rub.

She is still standing there staring at the eggs on the supermarket shelf; she has opened up the internet: At a push, a hen can lay one egg a day—but not always. It depends on the environmental conditions. On average, it takes 24 to 26 hours for a hen to produce, and this depends on the number of hours of light in an average female chicken's daily life, as for hens, light stimulates life.

Maybe that is where she and Jill went wrong. They were always in the dark.

She is on her banking app—she's trying to break it all down—all she does these days is check Jill's Insta or her banking app, flicking between the two screens: *banking, Jill, banking, Jill,* like a mad woman, to check either's transaction history.

The average female human will have all the eggs they will ever have at about 20 weeks of gestation; on hatching, they'll have 1-2 million eggs left, and by the time they hit their feelings, they'll have 300,000-400,000 eggs. In their reproductive years, one of these eggs should be ovulated each cycle, like the golden egg in fairy tales, for some, while 1000s of others are lost each month. Some say the lost ones die, but with body reabsorption, it could be argued that this process is, in fact, a form of reincarnation. The ovarian re-serve is like a bank, but it doesn't take deposits, and each month a woman withdraws from it, unsure of what she'll spend it on.

She has her hands outstretched towards the shelf; she isn't sure which box of eggs to select. How will she cook them? What will it cost to taste the runniness of their creamy yolk, looking like her mid-cycle wipe, once upon a time?

The fridge aisle has some hard-boiled eggs preserved in plastic, and on their label, it says, *no home freezing*, still, no cooking, so lower energy costs. But they don't look right to her somehow.

On the way to the supermarket, on the car radio, 3 DJs were talking about making eggs in an air fryer, and one had said, *you could incubate a child in that*, and laughed out loud, but she hadn't found it funny.

Her banking app is open again, £2.01p. The essentials range then. She opens the box and takes one out, holding it up to the light, which does not bounce off this low-quality egg, and she imagines it as one of her own, and she stares and stares at it and then takes it home, hidden under her arm, but never eats it, and secretly, she hopes that one day, it will hatch.

# THE ANTI-RED ROOM

The City is a crooked riad. The colour-coded barrier walls outlining the square mile have upper windows and balconies for the wall workers, designed to look back inward at the courtyard that is the City of London, but not outward. From the front, it's all castle and moat and drawbridge pulled up high. It is The Old City and it is The New City. It is The City reimagined as it always has been throughout history.

Except for this time, it has been reimagined for the few and with little pretence about it. Someplace just off Fleet Street, he asks her, *What's in that room?*

Virginia's eyes are fuses sparking. There comes a bored reply, *It's my anti-red room, nothing in there for you.*

She sees his forehead scrunching and relents. *Handicraft, I find it therapeutic.*

A shrug at his amused expression, and a robe is pulled over her long limbs as if to dismiss both him and his question; she is out of bounds now.

Harvey silently wonders, *What is it with women today?*

First, his wife, then his driver, and now her. There must be a full moon at bay. She-wolves in sheep's clothing, he imagines that if he were to put his ear close to their chests, he would hear their hearts howling.

*OwooooooOOOOoooooo.*

Harvey and his associates justify The City for the few as The City that could hold up the majority. Lessen the drowning, at least, throwing lifejackets here and there off one big luxury yacht. If only unhindered by the world outside its walls. Money had gotten them into this mess, and money could get them out of it. He at least lived off that promise. Though he understood the money would outlive him and any future life connected to him.

The City did not invent green finance; that much is true, but the few had positioned themselves as the centre of its universe. The world spun on its axis, continuing to revolve around The City, or so The City liked to think, spinning its plates at breakneck speed. And the plates span so fast that they bowled over the walls from time to time, and those beyond tried to catch them like seals on show at the sea life centre. *Clap,* catch, *Clap.*

A world-leading global centre had been dreamt up in order to attract the private funds needed to meet environmental salvage commitments. It had been a fantasy; the problem with fantasies, Harvey often thought, was that there was only so far you could go with them. Acting them out was one thing; fantasies you couldn't put back into Pandora's Box were another.

There were good guys and there were bad guys; he supposes he falls somewhere in the middle. Pulled left and right, more so right. It wasn't the first time a disaster had paved the way for dirty dollar. The City had been a corporation. A part of a bigger task force heavily targeting investments in green infrastructure projects: low-carbon transport, capital structure, from debt to equity, and, of course, the new-gen carbon cutters. The more desperate the world's rich became, the more the share prices shot up, and so the rich continued to feed the rich.

Beyond the walls of the riad, The City is a courtyard in full bloom: award-winning architects and planners and young green innovators have carefully implemented state-of-the-art greenage, low-carbon transportation and utility systems, and adaptable architecture around the square mile.

Harvey leaves his office on the top floor promptly after

his 11 o'clock meeting. As he makes his way toward the exit, the screens glow behind him like Christmas lights. A full house.

The glass elevator from the 200th floor is swifter than usual, as though it understands his need for speed. Mia is in the driver's seat, cloaked in huge sunglasses and head-to-toe in black, her usual uniform. She is a settler from California, and despite the heat, the uniform seems to serve as some kind of prolonged mourning period for a life she can never go back to.

*Where were you?* He asks, face twisting.

He isn't sure if he catches an eye roll from Mia in the review mirror, but the tint on her shades obscures the full truth from him. They pass the ruins of *St. Paul's Cathedral*, taking a turn down Fleet Street, past the former Sachs site, and then around the corner toward Virginia's apartment on Gough Square.

There were jobs inside The City for people like Mia and for people like Virginia. Those who pursued more creative options to secure a place. The few needed a reliable support network to ensure they could work at their optimal best. But they had to be sure it was a select support network.

There was a robust application system. Mia was from old US money, her family were major green shareholders, and she had achieved a perfect score on health and psychological profiling. Virginia had a PhD in Artificial Intelligence and Robotics and had also passed the screening tests with flying colours.

For the families of the few, no expense was spared. Wives, sometimes husbands, partners, and children were beyond pampered. Twenty-four-seven access to luxury temperature-regulated spas, offering over a thousand tangible nature sounds and senses, a refuge, high up in the clouds, almost. Ring-fenced, protected forest school patches for the kids, with insects that crawled there for them to wonder at, in managed mini-ecosystems, but time was one luxury the few could not afford to spare.

Harvey's own wife asks him that very morning about a holiday.

*We need a winter holiday*, she whines. *The children need some shade on their faces; it's been such a long summer. I feel like my bones are boiling.*

On a soft, wooden coffee table, a pile of bright, matte, recycled magazines lay. An advert for a luxury resort graces a front cover—a middle-aged couple stares dreamily into one another's eyes whilst holding children above their heads who are squealing with happiness—pine trees and tranquil lakes mist the background. A curved arrow of graphic text arches closely over the head of the blonde mother. It reads, *Families that vacay together, stay together*, as if it has been fired from a bow at her alone.

Harvey turns to his wife, about to address her demand, when a toddler soars into the air from the height of the back of a sofa.

*Wheeeeeeeeeeeeeeeeeeeeeeee.*

Careering toward the sharp edges of the white minimalist aircon unit, still minimally sharp enough to injure. Harvey catches the toddler just in time, an inbuilt reflex. As he wrestles with twenty pounds of pink wriggling flesh, the sleeve on his short dress shirt rides up against his barely built bicep, and his wife sees the mark. *What happened?* She seems concerned, almost.

His flesh is a shock to her, an unexpected intimacy. Their bodies are ghosts to one another beyond where tan lines would be if they tanned. But they don't.

*It's not her fault I don't want her anymore*, Harvey reasons.

Things went off rapidly in this climate. She was the mother of his children, after all, and there would be no more offspring. He smooths the reconstituted fabric back down, and the toddler, too, who is by now absorbed with a panel of screens. He bats a short answer back and leaves before it rebounds off the court wall.

Contact sport.


She is a reverse dress-up doll—she dresses things up, gives them a platform, she is good like that. Everyone, thing, wants to wear her and wear her over and over. She's intelligent, fluent in eleven languages, and funny to boot. Virginia can make you laugh on a bad day. That's important to him. She's good with money too, could have made it big in The City, he tells her. Virginia charges for all the extras— for things that don't even seem extra in the moment. She's had a top-class education, but that's not it.

Virginia questions the value of everything.

She has her own vigorous vetting process, and her clientele is select. Harvey waited twelve months to get onto her books. He thinks it was worth the wait. His negotiated package is bespoke, more cost-effective that way. Clearer boundaries for them both. Virginia caters to clients with all sorts of kinks: powerful men like him, men who want to be—

Harvey lasts much longer these days; he's developed little tricks to draw it out. The first time it had been all laid out on the bed, his loins had erupted into a throbbing frenzy, as though John Wayne had fallen against the electrical fences at The City walls, and he was caught vibrating, staggering. Over, Virginia unties the blindfold and places the paddle lightly on the bedside cabinet.

They lay side by side in a spooning position, his head burrowing deep into the soft curve of her neck and two hands holding her at her front, overfilling his splayed-out fingers and not swaying sideward as his wife's did.

Virginia would usually charge extra for this kind of intimacy, but he has it built in. Still, she has a soft spot for him, Harvey knows, Harvey thinks.

Her apartment scrapes the sky overlooking the Thames, and from their position, they can see it being held back like some inebriated bloke in a silly pub fight. The new bridge replaced all the bridges from Vauxhall right through to the former Greenwich foot tunnel. The inebriated bloke's mates—Lambeth, Westminster, Waterloo, Blackfriars, Millennium, and Southwark had formed a line like riot police, judicial brothers and sisters in interlinked arms, but were taken down with him, and now one big slab runs horizontally, concealing the former vertical tentacles of crossing and crossings.

Only the designated few make their way over this new lid of overbridge, like crabs trying to reach algae upon the shore. Circling shark fins scratch the ceiling of the bridge coffin, but they can't lift it; they have been buried alive with the bridges. Bridges where people had died; some by choice, some not. Bridges where people had pictures taken that were liked, bridges where people had professed love, and bridges where people had professed hatred.

Virginia looks up at him through a smog of smudged mascara, *You feel very needy today.*

She looks out toward the restrained river and back at him.

*You're holding onto my breasts like you don't want to go back to the office, like you're drowning, and they're buoys. They won't save you, you know.*

He slips back into his trousers like an eel. He leaves her a tip— a new high riser in the top twenty.

*I know you like to earn your money in other ways, but this is red hot. Don't say I never give you anything,* he touches his nose at her, a knowing salute.

The anti-red room is no such thing. Well, Virginia supposes it is, in a way, in the sense that it isn't all about the sexual gratification of her clients. It is a handicraft room. Sometimes clients tease that she's cloned herself, or versions of herself, to do her dirty work for her. The thought of it turns them on.

*Shake your chip at me, you dirty bitch,* one laughs.

Slaps her arse hard, makes amateur robot dance moves, and falls over himself in hysterics. One asks her to play the role; he takes the thought of it very seriously. He has her malfunction at the crucial moment. He's blown her away with all that he is, of course, he has.

*Malfunction, malfunction,* she says it so sweetly and robotically, just as he likes it.

They know all about her background, well, the key facts: education, health, likes, dislikes, measurements, house rules, and limits. And it's all technically true. She'd been involved in a top research project: *Uncanny Valley IX.* The stuff of breakthrough dreams. Virginia had won awards for her ideas. A poster girl for women in STEM, yes, still needed. She'd ended that marathon as a doctor of her sport, but as with all great things conquered, it hadn't turned out exactly as she had imagined.

Idealism was a killer, Virginia often said.

Virginia didn't sell sex for money. She sold sex for a chance at freedom.

There were versions of Virginia that were real, and there were versions of Virginia she constructed. Though who's to say what was real and what wasn't? She was a puppeteer of many selves, including all the selves she had never wanted to be.

She had loved her humanoids like the babies she would never have.

Sometimes she would dream of them at night; how they would look, the soft grooves of their newborn fingers, their first words. Models built on swatches of her sun-darkened skin, lab lights reflecting the patented pigment back at her. They were composed of childhood memories and folklore passed down from her female ancestors. They were her mother's perfume and her scalding words. They were conjured up from stories in history books. Stories that she wasn't sure were true.

The buzzer goes, and it's Howie; she smiles, watching him remove a helmet on the screen panel above her head. She has the night off. Well, Harvey is coming back around for seconds: a stressful day, but that won't take long. And then she can get back to herself, get back to the business of Virginia, to the final version.

She's hungry now and rips open the bag of food Howie is delivering, tearing off the paper and dropping globs of mealworm sushi into her mouth like oysters; her throat tipped back, but the mealworms don't slip down like oysters, and she mock chokes theatrically, and Howie laughs out loud.

He's not in the market, but they always have nice interactions, and that's something these days.

Howie leaves, and she flicks the channels idly, licking salty lab soy off her fingers. The camera pans to an interviewer who holds a mic under the nose of a silver-haired centenarian.

One of those, where were you on the day so and so happened anniversary programmes.

The man remembers being a small boy, so small he couldn't really understand why his grandpapa, his beloved Nonno, was crying. It was the day that Britain had finally decided to leave the EU, and The City had been forever changed.

*That's when the boundaries first began to shrink.* The interviewer nods.

They'd emigrated from southern Italy several decades before his birth, and his precious Nonno had worked his way

118

up from a small street stall to an upmarket gelato shop off Pimlico. Old Vincenzo had made it all himself by hand.

The silver-haired man's eyes are moist as he recalls his favourite flavour. He can see the hands of his Nonno beating cardamom, yolks, and sugar, his hands in free movement.

A tear runs down the mic, and it's taken away. The heirloom recipes had stopped there.


Harvey has been looking forward to this all afternoon; he is going to push her to push him. Test how far he can go.

Virginia has lain in wait, busying herself for his arrival. She has cleared the takeaway containers into the eco shoot. Looked at herself in the mirror, looked at all of herself and all of her selves. She has made comparisons: who was prettier, what was prettier. Lips pursed, the image in her mind only, she had never validated via selfies.

Harvey was late; he was always working late, the big buffoon, she thought.

It was no good for his health, having back-to-back meetings day in and day out, with no exercise apart from the little she gave him. No love, no affection, no fresh air.

There was no future for Harvey outside The City, all that money and all the holidays he could never take.

It wouldn't take long, she knew he'd been training himself, little tricks, she knew little tricks too.

He couldn't last long enough to inconvenience her plans that night. Virginia wouldn't allow it.

The buzzer noise is a tremble, a shrill of half notes; he must be nervous, she thinks, or overtired, good.

He takes his time coming up in the lift; she imagines his puffer fish lips shaped in a gormless O, checking the alerts on his device, loosening his overly tight waistband, and avoiding his own bloated reflection in the glass.

She becomes restless, she starts to feel drained with all the waiting; he is a tortoise.

He arrives. Falls through the door like a child who has been away on a school trip and missed its mother so. She undoes his tie slowly and tangles his hands with it behind him as he requests, binding the length of it over twice.

He's on his knees now, just as he likes it.

She asks him all about his day, *What has happened since this morning? Since his team briefing.*

*What happened with the new riser?*

He plays along, explaining the situation to her as though she were his most treasured client, his biggest investor. She has attached all of the restraints when she turns on her heel.

*Excuse me*, she says. *I'll be right back.*

Harvey follows the shadow of her limbs toward the bathroom door, but she strides right past, heading for the anti-red room, the space he's never entered. Her shadow disappears—she is the Peter Pan-ess of this new world; he told her that once. The little girl who never grew up.

His chest tightens, and he tests the firmness of the restraints; there is a stabbing pain somewhere between his shoulder blades. He's scared she won't come back.


*Come back, please, Virginia,* he pleads it silently.

There are pins and needles in his feet now, and he tries to shift his weight, but his body is topsy-turvy heavy. The door handle pops, and she is walking back out toward him, looking guilty.

*I am sorry*, she says. There was a bidding war, some materials for her handicraft hobby; it was important for her to get them, to be the winner.

She pats him down, retightening the ligatures in a soothing caress. *Just typical, now, where were we?*

Virginia has to coax herself through this one. She tells herself it is another version of herself, not the real Virginia.

Harvey is a sick man, she has decided. He is clamped from head to toe, and she has flogged him as hard as her strength will allow, every which way possible, at his demand.

She's got the vintage horse whip out now, and he tells her to say it to him. But she can't.

*Say it*, he pants, *say it*.

She talks to the control room in her head, *he is a sick, sick man*, she says. The control room agrees.

*Say it*, he shouts; he is getting angry, desperate now.

She rolls her eyes toward the sky, *just get it over with*, she tells herself, *just think of the payoff*.

She sighs, holding the whip at height above him; he's on all fours.

*Who's the bitch now?*

He groans in response.

*I am*, he's breathless, *I am*, he says.

His buttocks are serrated down the middle and the colour and texture of raw playdough.

*Say it again*, he begs.

Virginia cracks the whip a second time to the tune of his favourite fantasy.

As the whip comes down and he cries out, she hears the final neighs of all the horses that were sent to slaughter.

They're crying in her ears.

*Neighhhhhhhhhhhhhhh.*

His penis is standing all alone in the corner facing the wall, and he can't reach around himself crouched over this way, wrists burning. He is about to make a request when the whip comes down a third time, and she says something completely unexpected that makes it jump up like a jack-in-the-box, and the surprise is all on him. Sticky seed has made two new knee patches over his lowered work pants.

He is beet purple now. He tries his safe word, when that fails, the word, *Help*, is stuck in his strangulated chest. But Virginia does not hear.

Harvey thinks of his wife on their wedding night, how she had worked so hard to be the best version of herself for the occasion. At her ideal, ideal weight, teeth polished up like they'd never been used, and a spray all over her body mimicking melanin to look somewhere between herself and someone Other.

His chest is crushed raspberries.

Virginia had checked out some time before; she could be of no service to him.

As he lay there, she was touching down in paradise, enjoying the sensation of cool tarmac beneath her feet, and ready to feel the northern lights dance upon her face.

Some wonders never ceased.

Harvey remembers the births of all three of his children. How he had been there in that moment.

Virginia is swimming naked in a freshwater lake, and there is an oval of pine trees that smell like vanilla and guard her like a fairy ring.

She breathes in the oxygen from the pines with unadulterated glee.

Back in her luxury lodge, there are chips with enough data on to make a woman rich in ways that money cannot buy and a wardrobe full of all the selves she has selected.

Harvey's eyes roll like marbles across a children's playground and come to an abrupt stop over a shift in the way that the land lies. His eyes face the eyes of Virginia, who is also lying on the floor, arms all stiff from whipping, and with the spark gone from her fuses. She had left that one behind.

A moon rises up, up high over The City as a twinkling star, and it rises over the fairy pine ring and over Virginia too, and it is full now.

*OwoooooOOOOooooo.*

# OH, SPECIES
# OF THE TRANSPARENT HEART

After Italo Calvino and his *Cosmicomics*

*For the majority of Daphnia magna, or D. magna, environmental change holds little importance in the life of the members of a species since they cannot process or even really feel the effects of climate change – insofar as they do not take such matters to their little transparent beating hearts. At most, D. magna has only a vague perception of the actions (or inactions) of other individuals amongst the world's species and, in general, are very adept at adapting their populations to suit their surroundings, no matter what. And as such, it has been decided that they are the perfect specimens to study how species may cope with climate change. And all of this, they witness with one beady compound eye, safe in the knowledge that, for them, all the possibilities of evolution still lie ahead...*

# I

Long before me, roughly around 33.9 million to 23 million years ago, relatives of mine invaded the earth in the form of a small order of crustaceans: The Cladocera. Comprising around 650 species of water fleas—so-called due to our unusual hop-and-sink swimming style—no relation to our insect friends. We've more in common with a king prawn, garlic, and chilli linguine than those who inhabit dirty scratchy mutts. No, we leave parasitic activities to other species; our hop-and-sink mechanism simply allows us to make quick, impulsive jumps while we beat our antennae, propelling ourselves forward one body length at a time. And yes, we may look odd in our motions, but it gets us from A to B. During what I refer to as the sinking period, my personal favourite, we stretch out our antennae to increase our ability to drag our transparent bodies through clear bodies of freshwater, ensuring we don't entirely drown.

It's a thrill, really, living on the edge like that.

The balance of freshwater life depends on my species. It's both an honour and a huge responsibility, and quite honestly, I'd be very worried if it all fell into the wrong hands. You'd have no fish supper without our kind, at the other end of the spectrum, if we weren't around to eat all the algae... well then ... dead zones. That's right, zones of death. Read: not compatible with marine life and therefore life.

We, D. magna, love a bit of algae, and our filter-feasting acts like a kind of all-year-round algae bloom lawn mower without the energy costs. And without us, there would be an overgrowth of algae, and eutrophication would occur, resulting in hypoxic waters. Because most organisms need oxygen to live… few organisms can survive in such hypoxic conditions, attempt to adapt perhaps. When exposed to low oxygen conditions ourselves, we automatically increase our haemoglobin production, and our exoskeleton, our shell, made up of chitin and calcium (which is transparent as are many of our other organs), appears tinged with red due to the increased haemoglobin. Red stands for? So many things we cannot feel: anger, danger, love. We are the colour of our living conditions: when we feed on green algae, we appear transparent with a tint of green or yellow, whereas a snack of bacteria turns us white or salmon-pink to make the humans wink.

Our clear carapace makes us the perfect specimens for humans to watch and study our life processes in operation, a special kind of voyeurism. Can you imagine being able to see inside a heart without breaking it in some way? How it would be if, like me, your body was so truly naked that watchful eyes could see right through you and look straight into you, to the bottom of your heart and out through the other side. And see the beats, how fast they might go under manipulation. And all you can do is lie there, spread-eagled, bright lights dazzling your one good compound eye under a cover slide. D. magna hearts are at the top of our backs, just behind our heads—we wear our hearts tall—we make no attempt to hide our innermost workings. Our blood can be observed as it circulates, and our strange beating hearts pulse through our backs; odd to some, but the heart is the energy centre that drives life forward. And so, to our kind, it makes sense to have such an organ on our backs, propelling us forward through its force. While for other species, the way that they have the heart at the front, in the same direction they are expected to move forward, to feel, it almost seems like a design flaw. The force that comes from their hearts, dare I say, it makes them swim backwards.

Take the human heart, for instance: so close to the stomach, yet so near to greed. Below our heart is our brood chamber where we carry our eggs and young moving inside of our pouches, so close to love if we could feel such a thing. Asexual products (or at a push sexual) nestle within our shells like objects behind a looking glass in a natural sciences museum. In the perfect environment, mothers become daughters who become mothers who become daughters who become mothers, and on again, producing identikit clone versions of ourselves. In the ideal environment, we are free of entanglement, as there is simply no need for sex, males, or sperm. And what comes with sex is redundant: the male's hook is obsolete. In the perfect environment, our eggs are self-generating, as are we.

In our world, we only produce sexually when under environmental distress (and we also only produce males when under environmental distress). So, imagine a world in extreme environmental jeopardy—sex and men—and all of the conditions and contradictions that come with sex and men.

Under examination, at just twenty Celsius, our hearts may beat up to two hundred beats per minute, and you could watch this if you like; you could watch our little hearts speeding up under a cover slide. And you could take note of what happens to the hearts of a species under warming conditions, and then you could worry about what to do when you see the results. Through a Doppler, the sound of our warming hearts is something like a train chugging fast on tracks, think coal and rain beating down heavily on a tin roof, and it accelerates the hotter it gets. It's the kind of sound that human parents-to-be breathe a sigh of relief at in maternity hospitals at twelve-week and twenty-week scans, a heartbeat so fast it can hardly sustain itself. But its acoustic code means alive. And those mothers, they get to hold their babies, not always, but often. Whereas for our kind, after nurturing approximately one hundred eggs at a time, imminent death usually arrives in three to four days. But that's OK because we are never lost. In the perfect conditions, we will have produced multiple perfect identikit versions of our female selves, who will, in turn, in the ideal conditions, create multiple perfect identikit versions of our female selves. The males of our species are distinguished from females by their smaller size, larger antennules, modified post-abdomen, and first legs, which are armed with a hook used in clasping us... Yet we still dominate them in size and in many other ways too.

And what of me? Alas, I was not born into natural surroundings, as far as one can define natural, I suppose. I was born under laboratory conditions to study how species may cope with climate change. All I can say about this experience really is that under certain conditions, a D. magna's heart rate may increase to as much as three hundred beats per minute. And that at forty-eight Celsius, things can feel pretty balmy...

# II

*(We are all lined up as though on death row about to face a firing squad which is literally the fire of heat though simulated heat at that warmed to imagine the effects of climate change and how that could impact on other species the ruling ones and our bodies are in use to see how such species may or indeed may not adapt to increasing temperatures and so here we are all lined up next to one another side by side test tube by test tube and I'm first in the row test tube one and to my right I can see my clone sister basically myself and the test tubes we are all contained in are held up by a long horizontal piece of wire string that holds our death chambers firmly in place in a line inside the clear glass tank with the buttons on the side that the white coats press that makes the temperature go up and they can see us all with some of us fainting before death through the transparent glass of the tank and through this clear glass they can see through the clear containers of our bodies and through these bodies they can see through our translucent fast beating*

*hearts and some pass out six to twelve times on average before they succumb and my heart it goes faster and faster the hotter it gets and they need to see how fast it can beat until it can beat no more due to the heat and so they turn the dial up and up and whatever number it gets to when I die they'll be mindful I'm sure to try not to let things get that hot for themselves or their own kind to determine what's the cut-off point for devastation?)*

# III

...Which doesn't mean that the cut-off point for the white coats devastation was automatically ours too, as largely, for us at least, the many possibilities of evolution still lay ahead, or indeed would adapt to suit us or vice versa. Of my own birth, I was the product of cultured clones spanning across two generations. To protect myself, or rather the experiments around myself, from the risk of maternal effects and avoid the traits my mother could have passed on (if I'd had one in the truest biological sense), and so I was twice removed from her population-wise. I noted that such experimentation had been solely created with the idea of how a species could adapt to human-caused environmental change, and through the human-controlled experiment at that. Spinoza had said: In nature, there is nothing contingent, but all things have been determined from the necessity of the divine nature to exist and produce an effect in a certain way. And I'm attracted to this idea and curious—but I'm powerless to consider it further in the context of myself, for I have no control over such matters. Or do I?

No matter what, I can say I was the first (or amongst a batch of the first) D. magna studied in order to document evolutionary changes in the thermal tolerance of natural populations as a response to recent temperature increases—and parental detachment issues aside—that's quite a claim to fame.

# IIII

Afterward, the world often seemed meaningless without them. Though in some ways, it was brighter. You could really see things for what they were since the fall of the controlled environment and those who had once dwelled within it. We luxuriated in thermal lakes and ponds after changing our genetics to tolerate the higher temperatures—and they had been right—we could easily adapt to, say, a four Celsius rise in temperature biannually. There had been years of war and contention, though. At points, we had been left with no option but to grow helmets, spikes, and crests in response to the chemical cues and signals that predators were near, those brought even closer to us through the changing climate. As I speak now, I talk not through my former voice or former self but through my newly evolved self. All at once: I am myself, my offspring, my clones, separate and not separate, entangled only by my own determination. I am the voice of my children, my sister, my mother, and I, we, evolve, adapt, and on we go, and on it all goes. It's all cyclic, as it should be.

Yes, at points when our environment was under significant threat, we had to endure sex and men (and all of the conditions that come with sex and men). And yes, we still laid resting haploid eggs just as a precaution, in case we ever needed to mate to carry our species on under dire circumstances (in short, we D. magna will invest in sexual reproduction when its relative costs are reduced). It's not the simplest way around things, though, or is it? And just occasionally, we thought of the humans... and our little transparent beating hearts... carried on as normal.

# And how did that make you feel?

Date: 22nd April, 20—

FAO: American Psychiatric Association (APA)

**Enclosed**: Copy of transcripts and session analysis as supporting evidence for the proposed revision of the forthcoming DSM—X—TR (®)

This letter refers to what some have perceived as controversial changes to the DSM (Diagnostic and Statistical Manual of Mental Disorders), particularly the latest edition due for publication: the DSM—X—TR. In response to your callout earlier this year in Therapy Today (Volume 120, Issue 6), please see enclosed copies of some notes and transcripts drawn from my therapy work associated with 'eco' related mental disorders. I, for one, fully support the proposed inclusion of new mental disorder classifications and codes in the forthcoming edition, and I am pleased to be able to add to the growing body of evidence demonstrating that the climate crisis has unleashed mental disorders never witnessed before. I fully support that this calls for new classifications across psychiatric and psychotherapeutic counselling fields.

Incidentally, I still agree with some critics that 'medicalising' mental health must be avoided within the DSM as a whole. However, I believe that recognising certain disorders caused by environmental uncertainty will enable those affected to receive more rapid and appropriate help and serve as a record of these significant times of change occurring in climate and human history.

Yours Sincerely,

Gaia Albrecht, (BACP, BPS)


**[Records of transcripts provided for evidence]**


Transcript guide: C = client T = therapist S =supervisor (numbers e.g. 1) = pause in seconds

Cl: He said I had wasted all my heartbreak. That I could've really made something out of it. Use it—he had said, just like that. (3)

T: Use it? How so?

Cl: I wanted to be a writer and heartbreak (2) – true heartbreak – offers that kind of raw emotion which takes you to a place you can't access in everyday life. And I had missed a trick, according to him—a few tricks.

T: How did it make you feel? When he said that?

Cl: At the time?

T: Yes, or any time.

Cl: Like a failure, like I'd failed at love and then failed to use that failure. He had turned one of his breakups into a greatest hit – played it on request at funerals and weddings after troubling the charts – that's proactive. (4)

T: Mmm::

Cl: It's honouring what was lost, at least. Less wasteful. (3)

T: Given your past relationship, how did it feel receiving advice from him?

Cl: I don't know, I mean, I think he was genuinely trying to be helpful— (4)

T: Mmm::

Cl: Half of me wondered why I hadn't had enough of an impact on him to have a song written about me when we were together (2) Sorry, that's childish and going off-topic.

T: Would you like to explore it further?

Cl: No, no, it's insignificant.

T: Mmm::

Cl: Really, I was immobilised by grief, and I felt I was too despondent to apply myself in that way at the time. Now look at me. It's too late. (5)

T: Perhaps you could have used the experience to draw

from later if you wished. You still could. (2)

C1: You can't. Everyone knows that— (2)

T: Mmm::

C1: You have to do it while you're riding it – or rather whilst it's riding you. It's that pendulum that swings so violently between grief and love – and being on either end of its extreme is like existing on a different plane from everyone else. You really go somewhere— (3)

T: Mmm::

C1: You can recall it, the memory. But the searing grief – the surges – it's like a genie. You can't just resummon it at will. I suppose it is like childbirth in a sense, and we block it out. Otherwise, we'd never go through it again.

T: How do you feel the impact of grief affects you in your life now? (3)

C1: It's something I witness every day, with funerals, especially the mass ones. (2) The mourners, when they come – it's a day they think will be indelible in their minds. They make promises to themselves they'll never keep – how precious life is, their loved ones, and how it's made them realise. (3)

T: Mmm:

C1: The finality, and that reminder of mortality— (2) it

blows their lives up on a big screen— Don't get me wrong, for a small number, I'm sure life will never be the same again. But for most, it's just a zoom-in, then zoom back out to a comfortable view again once the day is over. (4)

T: How does your job role affect you? Do you feel?

C1: I see people now, more than I see myself. And although I call myself a humanist celebrant, I really consider myself more of a multi-species celebrant. I call other animals back to life by honouring them in the services, but I think they should be buried alongside the humans and should be remembered and revered the same way (3). It's becoming problematic—

***

C2: I can understand why some men kill their children—

T: You understand I have to break confidentiality if I believe a person or persons may be at risk?

C2: Oh, I don't mean me, mine, just (4) you see it on the news, and you think, how could they do it? And I just think we often see the worst parts of ourselves reflected in our children. So perhaps, in that moment, it's not the child they're trying to kill.

T: Can you say more? (3)

C2: Since my wife left, I – I don't know – (3) I seem to have more empathy with men. I've never been one of those guys who goes to the pub after work, in fact, I'd be hard pushed to say I had a friend to call on. I just feel like now (4), even though so much is literally right out of our hands – they still expect men to be able to exert control – to reign things, even themselves, back in again.

T: And how do you view yourself? Your role? (3)

C2: I just feel like she wanted so much from me. Like I wasn't enough, for her, for our kids. They were asking me to crack an impossible code – (3) I wanted to protect them—

T: Do you want to take a moment?

C2:

T: Feelings can be very powerful.

***

S: Have there been any sessions in particular that are acting as a trigger for you feeling this way?

T: All of them, and none of them. I don't know if it's me— (3) if I'm just reading from them what I want to—so I can reassure myself that I'm not the only one. But it's unnerving – it's like seeing a big ball of thread become loose, and it's getting so tangled. And the more tangled up people become in it, the more anxious they get, and the tighter it pulls.

S: Mmm::

T: It's like a mass hysteria – but at the same time, you wonder if it's the opposite of that (4) a completely rational mass mental and emotional response to what's been happening. Like our brains have finally evolved to catch up. (4)

S: So, are you having trouble distinguishing between the traditional transference you might experience in client work, or are you trying to say that this is something new, more significant, like a phenomenon?

T:

S: Sorry, you don't have to answer that. (5)

T:

S: I've been seeing it too. Whispers::

***

C3: He says he loves me, but I feel like he doesn't respect my values. He keeps asking me for things that go so far against what I believe in. And he knew from the start.

T: And how does that make you feel?

C3: Sad, lonely (4) and lost. Frustrated most of all—and I feel so angry (3) I'm not a nice person to be around. I have hate in my heart. I wake up with it in my mouth every morning and spit it in the sink. I'm not sure why he thinks I'd make a good mother—

T: And how does that make you feel? (3)

C3: Well, that's not relevant.

T: That's OK. I just wondered if you wanted to explore further because you made a reflection there, and you mentioned in the past, aside from the environmental impacts, that a lack of a mother figure—

C3: No, that's not it—My decision is purely based on being a good human being, a good citizen, on not being selfish. (2) And why would anyone want to bring a child into a world like this, even if the will was there?

T: Mmm::

C3: I just don't understand it. He's so educated. In every other way, he's so switched on.

T: Mmm::

C3: His job is at the forefront of sustainability. For Christ's sake, he knows, he knows! But he wants to have a baby, and he thinks it will be an extension of us when it's all over. But it's already over.

T: How do you feel you might overcome the difficulties in the relationship in the future?

C3: I just think he needs time to think, to change, to become a more rational person. You know he thinks I'm irrational—

***

T: Welcome to the session. First of all, I think it would be a good idea if we could just go around in a circle and check in with how we are all feeling today. (5)

C4(a): I don't really want to say anything. I don't want to be here.

T: Well, I'm glad you felt able to share that. Thanks for being so open and honest.

C4(b): I just, I—I'm sorry, God, I'm crying already. (5) I just don't see why she can't try. It's like I'm the only one who is really trying to fix things in this family.

T: That's OK, it's important to honour feelings and all be heard – (2) there are some tissues on the table in the centre. Please help yourself. (3)

C4(c): Well, I don't mind being here because I want to

support Mum. And Dad, I suppose. I just find it all kind of awkward, but it's OK.

T: Thank you for sharing. (2)

C4(d): Well, I can't say I'm a natural at this either—but we need something. We can't go on feeling like this. It's not sustainable. It's like in our house, there's this thick fog, a depression like nicotine dripping down the walls.

T: Mmm::

C4(d): Since we had to move away—there's been this sense of something that I can't quite put my finger on. We've only moved counties, and we are not really affected by it here – but it's the uncertainty that's hard to live with.

T: Mmm::

C4(d): It affects our moods, the kids' moods. I mean, I know they are teenagers (3), but they shouldn't be living with this level of angst.

T: Mmm:: (2)

C4(b): I just really feel like we're not relating to one another (3), and that's where it's all broken down.

T: Mmm::

C4(b): I mean, that's why they call it a relationship, isn't it – you're meant to relate to one another. But they're in their rooms, and he's on his device, we don't speak over dinner, and it's just this horrible, awful atmosphere, and I feel so guilty— (5) I'm sorry—

T: Do you want to take a moment?

C4(b): Cries::

C4(a): Well, she keeps carrying on like this all the time, constant wailing—

C4(d): Honey, let's not—

C4(a): No, Dad, she does. And it's catching. The misery. It's contagious. You were right. I think that she should come for therapy on her own. I'm not being rude, but Mum, you are really the one with the major issues here—and everyone else is just trying to get on with things and doing their best to shut it all out.

C4(b): [Shutting it out! Exactly, can't you see that's half the world's problem?!]

T: Right, well, I think it's healthy to voice difficult feelings (7) to make the most out of therapy, perhaps we could look at some structured ways of reflecting on the issues at hand—

***

T: How have you been feeling since our last session? You had been dealing with some displacement and dissociation issues? (7)

C2: My old boss said relationships are like battleships, made for sinking. Pretty soulless, right?

T: Mmm::

C2: He had a point, though. There's only so long they can stay afloat (5), and the way you go down makes all the difference. For me (3), my problem was the style in which I sank.

T: Can you say more? (4)

C2: I just felt like I'd been removed from everything, and like everyone had been removed from me (2) I felt place-less—

T: Mmm::

C2: That sounds kind of strange because by virtue of being alive, we always have a place, we are central to place – it's central to us (5). I don't know, I just felt— (3)

T: Yes—

C2: Like I was experiencing some bizarre disconnect. Like the world was spinning around me, and it was a ride I was stuck on— and I didn't trust the safety bar—

***

S: How have you been feeling since our last session?

T: In some ways, good. I feel like I've been able to help a

lot of people who are really just struggling to make sense of what they're feeling more than anything. (6)

S: And the transference, the uneasiness we spoke of last time, have you reflected on this or noticed any shifts at all? (3)

T: I suppose one thing, something a mother said in a family session— (3)

S: Mmm::

T: That some of their problems lay in not being able to relate to one another— (3) and I suppose if we can't relate to one another (2) or at least try – how can we solve a universal problem that belongs to every single—

****

C1: I've been thinking, being a celebrant, it's a close second to being a writer, actually. (3)

T: Mmm::

C1: I mean, what I write has been given to me – you work from facts (3) – but you have to make it into something else. And for most people, their everyday lives are just mundane. And my job is to dig out the good stuff—show humanity at its best during a period when it is still recovering from having been at its worst. (5)

T: So—

Cl: So maybe all the heartbreak hasn't been wasted after all. (3)

T: Have you been reflecting on this since our last session?

Cl: Laughs:: (10)

T: [Do you]—

Cl: I have. (2) One of the key things—and I kind of mocked people for this before—is that at the funerals, people always intend to make some kind of change, and in some cases, grief can pave the way for transformation—

T: Mmm::

Cl: Whereas with weddings, it's about new starts – or consolidation – the first flush of love (or second or third or fourth), a commitment to another aside from oneself, following a framework (4), and I don't know if that can set people up to fail—

T: Mmm::

Cl: But in one sense, maybe we need frameworks for love more than ever—perhaps they could be more diverse, though. (2)

T: Mmm::

Cl: As a humanist, though I don't know if I can call myself that for much longer… Sighs:: (2) without feeling like a hypocrite. We often speak of the circle of life. Instead of religion, we point out our similarities with the natural world around us to offer comfort when a life comes to an end— (Client uses hands to demonstrate circles)

T: Mmm::

C1: The end comes for us all, like the seasons— (2) and traditionally, this metaphor has helped those who have suffered loss to understand, to process.

T: Mmm::

C1: And now I'm just really struggling (3) I can no longer say (2) don't be afraid, in winter the flowers may die, but in spring they will be reborn again, that life and death are natural cycles, I can't offer the same reassurances—

***

C4(a): I'm only fifteen, but even I can see that she needs medication, not talking therapies. Half the street is on them. It's the norm.

C4(b): [Half the street is being numbed, subdued, blinded.]

C4(a): Who is the teenager here, Mum? Why don't you

give me a chance to speak? I actually wish you and Dad would get divorced so I could go and live with him.

C4(b): [Be careful what you wish for.]

T: How have you all been feeling about the issues raised since the last session?

C4(c): I just feel like most of the tension is between them two—I know I don't always help and sometimes they feel like I'm siding with one or the other, but sometimes there's just no need (3) we can still live an OK life, compared to some—

T: Mmm::

C4(d): [I think your mother just wants the best for you] for both of you—we both did (2) do, but things have changed, and we are struggling to cope with the lives we have led you into... (3)

C4(c): But that's not helpful, Dad. On top of all the other struggles we have to deal with you and Mum, I just feel like we could do something to get rid of the misery (3) maybe we could look to others, try and help those who are actually worse off than us. (2)

T: Thank you for sharing your feelings (2) is there a way you could all move forward based on the things you have shared today?

C4(d): It's not as simple as that—it's not a feeling you can just push away—it's like it is happening to you in slow motion—

***

C3: I sat with him for hours and hours, and I really do love him so much. He is just the only person who really gets me. (4)

T: We've spoken before about emotional dependency, and you indicated that this is a barrier for you moving on. How do you feel about that now?

C3: On one hand, you could say I'm emotionally dependent on him (4) because I can't imagine a future without him, because he's all I have ever known. But is that unhealthy, or just simply natural?

T: Mmm::

C3: Part of me thinks I'm being self-centred, he wants a family, and I can't offer him that, but then I mentally override my part in contributing to our issues (4) because I believe that he is selfish for wanting children, and so my role in our unhappiness should be overlooked. (2)

T: Mmm::

C3: But, deep down, I know I'm not fulfilling him. If I put this out to the masses, online or whatever, they'd call him out, not me (4), but on a one-to-one level, I know I'm letting him down. Maybe I'm a coward. (3)

T: What makes you feel that way? (10)

C3: Something we spoke about a while ago (2) the abandoned child syndrome thing—

T: Mmm::

C3: I suppose I do struggle with the idea of permanence, of being someone else's gauge for stability, a straight line to follow. I just wish they had told me she was ill—yes, I was too young to remember, but because of what they did, how they did it, I don't remember. (4)

T: Mmm::

C3: I don't remember feeling or processing it – it's always just been stuck. And I'm scared— (2)

T: What are you scared of?

C3: I'm scared of those I love leaving me and never coming back, and I'm scared of leaving them too—

***

T: I am worried for them. But I don't want them to see it. In my face. It's getting harder. (3)

S: Mmm::

T: The thing is, I don't think some of the anxiety they're experiencing is unnatural—or, you know, linked to other stuff for them. (2) And I guess I'm concerned that encouraging them to look deeper within is distracting them from what's right in front of them. I feel responsible—

S: You realise it's not your responsibility to change or redirect their thought processes? You can help them self-reflect. It's up to them to reach conclusions—

T: [But what if they're concluding the wrong things?]

S: There is no such thing as wrong per se. Their experiences and interpretations of their own issues are valid and—

T: [But I feel I have this one great chance]

S: Mmm::

T: To make people realise—to make that connection to how they're feeling with what's been going on, and yes, I know people have always lived with uncertainty— (4)

S: And how does it make you feel? You seem to be conflicted between your role as a psychotherapist and your role as—

T: [I'm not saying I have any special kind of role] (2) I know I'm no different than the next therapist. I'm not even published on any of these issues directly… and so many are, and I could— (4)

S: How would it make you feel? If you did have your voice heard? Externally? (3) Say through publication or some mode outside of client work and supervision? (5)

T: I don't know—I've published before on so many subjects (3) but saying this out loud, putting it down on paper—

S: Mmm::

T: Deep down, I'm not sure what I'm seeing – the patterns – I'm not sure that (2) I want to believe it's all true. Perhaps (3) I have some sort of disordered thinking myself, or maybe it is transference or both, or maybe it could all be—

S:

# THE LIGHT OVER THERE

*In the summertime, the lake starts here.* The fisherman tells this to the two off-season tourists, a couple, as he guides the boat. They are a few miles out on Lake Skadar in Montenegro by now. He is smoking close to the diesel engine, and the woman tourist looks uncomfortable. She shifts her body towards the other end of the boat, by around an inch to the right, with each drag the fisherman takes until there is almost no boat left her side.

The fisherman wonders what she is scared of the most, but he doesn't ask. Fire or drowning or fire and drowning, he wonders. Instead, he asks if she can swim, like the birds and the fish. The fisherman knows all about fires because the fisherman is a fireman too. He is in communion with the water and the things that swim beneath or on top, and with fire and the things that leap and hiss.

Finally, the fisherman flicks his cigarette.

He has learned to hold all of these environments in his bare hands. The fish try to jump through his fingers. The flames try it too. Though slippery and hot, he holds them gently but firmly and whispers to them, *You are safe here*, or, *You are not safe here, go.*

In the distance, a small breeding colony of Dalmatian Pelicans senses their approach. Wings silently start to move, to retract, to bend back into themselves as though they are extinct. Play pretend. Their numbers were dwindling, though, for sure. The birds notice the aura of the woman tourist and decide to grant her wish, stopping still instead of flying far away. They are very intuitive.

The fisherman turns the engine off and slowly lets the boat glide towards the majestic creatures still in their eyeline, for now. The silence is so much. Emotions circle high overhead and then surround the three humans like an unseen tornado. All are stock still, should there be a predator amongst the flock. The fisherman, the tourists, and the Dalmatian Pelicans all adopt somewhere between the freeze pose of prey and apparent death.

Sunshine has travelled from the light they first spotted across the lake on the Albanian side at the start. Crossing the transboundary of the wetland. It makes the birds' white-silver heads dazzle brilliantly like diamonds. A liquid gold runs off the edges of the woman's hair and makes it seem as though her hair has caught fire, but it hasn't. She still feels the heat as if in anticipation.

The fisherman doesn't realise this, but the woman tourist is scared of something else. Of things coming to an end before she gets the chance to figure out the end for herself. How will she know? If she is really loved? If the boat goes down or the flames torch her locks.

Three days a week, the fisherman works down at Bar, fighting the wild ones. Because sometimes the Adriatic doesn't swell high enough to douse them. Then two days a week, he's on the boat showing tourists the lake up on Skadar, as far as Montenegro goes, before it reaches the Albanian border with its nose. On the other days, the fisherman just floats around the lake with his boat in total serenity.

The season was all skewed now, but in the old season, tourists could see water lilies, greens, yellows, and whites laid out like a magical carpet, and eat chestnuts right off the water, watching the Dalmatian Pelicans and sometimes their silent, graceful movements, if they were lucky.

With the engine turned off, the man tourist tries to command the silence further and asks for complete silence so as not to disturb the silence. *No talking, please*, he says to the fisherman and the woman tourist with a smile. He records the silence on his mobile phone, and the fisherman and the woman hold their breath as he does so. He holds his phone up and angles it out towards the lake, recording all its invisible boundaries and edges, and finally, he captures the Dalmatian Pelicans. Their graceful but strong necks, huge bills, gizzard pouches, orange hues, heavier than swans' bodies, and wingspans stretching out far enough to rival the Great Albatrosses. Lastly, he zooms his lens in to focus on their grey plumage, so soft they look like they are made of spun silver.

The Dalmatian Pelicans mate with one partner with whom they share a nest, a life, and migrate with for several breeding seasons and, in some rare cases, forever—taking it in turns to incubate the female's eggs. When the fisherman is able to talk again, he tells the tourist couple all of this. They had both migrated from different borders, and the fisherman sensed a tension or something difficult, and it made the boat rock gently. It is the fisherman's job to keep the boat stable.

*The light looks so beautiful over there. Can you cross the border to reach it?* The man tourist had asked at the start. The fisherman replied, *Yes, but you'll end up in prison. It's illegal to cross the border of the lake, even if the border is unmarked. Only the Dalmatian Pelicans can fly over the border for free, but even they pay a price.* They had all looked towards the light over there.

As they were about to depart again, a noise on the lake made all on the boat turn and look. The Dalmatian Pelicans were spreading their wings, in and out, in and out, wider with each motion, as though in dance, like ballet dancers, and the silence in the air was the music of Tchaikovsky.

Their breeding rafts, created to combat the man-made floods and pollution, acted as a wide dance stage, and they pirouetted in perfect synchrony.

You see, said the fisherman, *We just need to restore the balance.*

# HIDE

*Bless me, Father, for I have sinned.* Tomás hears movement from behind the other side of the oak screen. *Flapping.* He lifts his head. Whole being still now, prey, shoulders, and neck are frozen. Chest facing forward. Heart hammers. The resultant pulsations seemingly send a ripple right through the water out in front of the bird hide. Fear and courage both spin away from him. They are the same stones in his pocket. They hit the water in a straight flat line, a successful skim.

Like a heron on one leg, full of grace and topped with blue-silver, his head, Tomás turns so slowly. Common reeds grow planck length into golden brown from creeping rhizomes underground in the time it takes for him to rotate his head fully. He looks to his right to see who has answered him. *Kek, kek kek*, sings the voice. Followed by a ruffle sound, then, *Kek, kek, kek.*

Tomás begins again. Adjusting to the environment. *Forgive me, Father, for I have sinned. My last confession was seventy years ago, and these are my sins*—as he makes the sign of the cross, an army of black-tailed godwits, curlew, wood sandpipers, and greenshank advance.

Through the hide's front viewing window, the leader, a black-tailed godwit, has a criss-cross of worms in its mouth mimicking Tomás.

There are three of the creatures in a row, swimming in his direction. Tomás watches them, playing for time. In his head, they are the O'Flaherty brothers at Sunday mass, and he is right back there. On collection duty, waiting for their show to finish. Puffs of big white sleeves sashaying down the altar catwalk. Carrying smug faces, special objects, and the smell of incense, all overpowering. And special treatment that would stay with them.

He remembers the voice of Father from the other side of the screen, the last and only time he made confession. But Tomás had not been believed, and so he lost his faith. There are two types of people who come to a place like this. Those who are wishing away the present and those trying to claw back the past. His new feathered Father encourages him now to change his camera lens to a wide-angle. Tomás removes the strap from his shoulder, and with a *click*, he changes his view. He is being asked to look at the bigger picture.

The two types of people had jostled in the queue to get in, each group wary of and rolling eyes at the other. A large man in a mac with a camera lens longer than any beak in here had nearly crushed a small child, driven there to make memories. Family memberships. A formal extension of trying to belong somewhere, together, paid by monthly direct debit. He remembered those days. Then there were men here like him, singular but bound together, waiting one another out.

Tomás was happy that hides could be pre-booked these days, so he and his type could take turns trying to look through their lenses at varying focal points. Less grunting. Ears pricked up like a dog, he listens and hears the sound of waiting and wings. The time clock is ticking on his membership app. At a wide angle, he has a lot to be sorry for. But he can also see some good from this perspective. And he just wants to be absolved. *I am sorry for all the sins of my past life,* he says, head bowed.

The hide is a new eco one built with funds donated by a former volunteer who had died and lived longer than he had hoped. His wish was for those who have to look longer and harder than they wanted to be able to do so from a comfortable viewing spot. Snippets of natural beauty thrown in.

Situated at the wood-end marsh area of the reserve, remaining passage waders still arrived in autumn and spring. Some salmon hues of protected pink-footed geese could be seen in winter. Tomás examined his conscience more fully, adjusted his lens a little wider, *I am sorry to have stolen so much in my life.*

*A ruffle.*

Birds display such empathy. And anger and fear. Love and joy. Some mate for life. They can be good listeners. Sunlight bounces off the reedbed, and there is a porthole window to the right-hand side of the hide, which passes through the wetland to the past. The melodic voice sits behind it, calling Tomás to continue and proceed with his confession. *Kek, kek, kek.* Musical call claiming its territory, a higher rank. The one in a position to enable forgiveness or not, the bird could not speak for its entire species; it could only act as a gatekeeper between Tomás and a higher power. *Kek, kek, kek.*

He had stolen many things throughout his life: chocolate, his own time, others' time, love, money. Tomás was not terribly ashamed of the above. He could live with those actions, put them down as par for the course of living. Other things, though, he could not sit well with. With his lens on

this requested wide-angle, things were not so well magnified, though, and so he could avoid it. He understands why
the bird asked this of him, to start things off gently. Tomás
feels he does not deserve such compassion.

The old Father had made him start with the hardest
things first, tough love. Dished out a penance, twelve Hail
Marys, and a clip around the ear after for even thinking,
believing, such things may happen in his lifetime, and that
he might be a part of it. He looked him square in the eye as
he took the collection pouch off him the Sunday after and
said, *Child, if you think bad things are going to happen, then
they will. Be careful what you think.* And so, after that, for a
long time, he tried not to think at all.

A *beep-beep* noise comes from his app, and he sees the
digital clock symbol in single figures. Another noise, the
shuffling and whining of the other type of people waiting
for their turn outside. A toddler's cry. Tomás can't remember
what it is like to be so small, so reliant on those bigger than
you, whose every decision impacts the rest of your life. To
buy you a single or twin cone ice cream, the health of your
teeth, sherbet, and sauce, or just sauce. To stay together or
not, two school bags, at two houses, split your favourite ted-

dy in half, lose its scent, or not. To bury their head in the sand or look up. To teach you how to do the same or not.

There is a small *kerfuffle* behind the other side of the oak screen now, and Tomás hears his counsel give an alarm call. They, too, have heard the approach of a ground enemy, and so the call is pertaining to that, *Kek, kek, kek*, not the quieter alarm call given to an aerial predator. They have a special language to warn of those who travel by foot. The feathered Father puffs out a brown-grey breast and quickly signals to Tomás to change his lens one more time, to the telephoto lens. To bring scenes and subjects much closer.

*Click.*

There is a small child's foot against the door. Impatient pushing, on his app, time ebbs away, down to seconds. A lower alarm call from the other side of the screen, *Kek, kek, kek?* His eyes can barely focus.

He can hardly bring himself to sharpen the perspective. But he does, and he sees it all in high definition. There are two doors to the hide, so one doesn't have to pass by the other. One entering this world as one leaves, a squeal at the view is emitted as Tomás's foot steps out into the hot sun, his voice leaving behind an echoing whisper. *The future, forgive me.* And the gatekeeper flies away.

# Snow star

Only the elders understand where all my white has gone and why. Rocks and rocks left. I was mourned until their last breath, their spirits soaring to greet me. And I returned water and life unto each one. To the believers whose faith was not enough in the first life.

Black hooded cloaks and whispers. *Who, what is talking?* I have already departed in form, physically. Watching from above. I am all around them. Encircling as the funeral procession climbs over the tip of the sacred mountain. Fire elements follow.

Quickening heat at their heels. They want to mark what my absence means. I count them at over a hundred, not enough to mark my lifetime, but mark it they do.

Some small form of activism. They lay a wreath on the now grey. One reads a eulogy.

Underneath, at the bottom of where I was, a plaque reads:

*Dear Future, this monument acknowledges that we are aware of what is happening and what needs to be done. Only you know if we did it. Followed by the date.*

***

The young make their pilgrimage each year, though I am still lost. They have to play make-believe.

*Qoyllur R'iti*, they call out.

Their motions with the ice pick are merely symbolic, and they carry pre-frozen blocks of ice in a freezer attached to their trucks. Once they descend, *hack, hack*, and each group of pilgrims is handed a faux block to return with to their settlement. The carving chunks out of me had become a ritual—a symbol of water and life. The pick dug deep in my belly until the government forbade it.

*Plastic pagans*, I call them now.

Though the final lessening of me came not from them. Their forebears took the ice too.

Some were just superstitious, thought that by carrying me, I would be a penance for their sins. Or that my melt-water could cure the incurable. They came before, high up on me, in woollen masks and furry cloaks split down the middle with the sign of the cross. Blood red and warmed in the cold by it. And their children's children still wore the same costume to carry on tradition, but most fell now with the hot.

Though I have receded, it is said Apu lives on. They believe, as they have always believed, that I am awake and conscious, their protector, as is Mother Earth. Each year on the Winter Solstice, by the light of a full moon, they trek. Stopping in every village along the way to dance, pray, and sing. Though the snowfields reserved for the rituals are turned to mud now.

The plaque on the rock marks the spot—the first great white to turn into a puddle.

And there was one who led several processions – from festival to funeral – and when I fell, he fell too.

Mariano had receded, and all around him had lessened. Though he prayed to the gods, day and night, and his data too. Just two tufts of hair left and two teeth. He had been a modern man, though accepted by his people. He never fully left the village—a man of science and spirit. His news was not wanted, and some blamed him and his family for the changes when the plaque to the future became a memorial to the present.

The elders had put their hands together in prayer and asked him to join them and consider how he could keep faith in Apu when he kept so close to science.

How could they perform a miracle?

Three beds in Mariano's small house had become one after she left and took his children with her. And the house itself shrank as the heat walls dried, the mud thinned and thinned. And the birds no longer roosted on the roof—nest nor nook no more.

In the casket, his body was wasted. Not prettily plumped up under the shroud by undertakers—fluids scarce—but shrivelled. He was freeze-dried. Shrunken and subtracted. Two children, and a dead wife he never divorced. One child had had four children, and they had three each, so that, with only two of his children's children living, that made the split of his estate go fourteen ways.

Unravelled, they decided it would be best to turn his history into a museum of memory. For the man that called out, *Qoyllur R'iti*. To warn of the way ahead. And the people would pay to visit, and they would earn more out of their inheritance that way. Preserving the pre-melt past.

Once inside, a 6D light display would project faux white ice layers over the mountains just behind Mariano's former home. For those who wanted the ultimate experience, they could flick their chip and be way up high. An Ukuku for real on the tip of a sacred glacier. A chance to go back in time and no longer bargain for the elements but take just enough. With a blessing from Snow Star too. Oh, how it would feel to be blessed. One room draws the most visitors, empty but for a standing desk, a vintage Mac device, and a digital reader holding the holy data.

As a nice departing touch, a machine would shoot cold air on the way out before getting back on the tour boat, and people could close their eyes, inhaling deeply and imagine that all they could see was white.

Apachita, as a young girl, walked six hours up my old spine tied to her father's back. To play a game where carrying on rituals meant something could last forever.

Or was it a second funeral parade, not for me but for them?

Apu signalled fertility, and so it was important for little women to run amongst my grave. She would grow up and out, nine months wide. Growing a wedge and a thickening just as I once did, only to shed it with sorrow and then grow another layer. Would she go on to have the life force within forced out—with an ice pick—and on and on. For whom? What? With a belly full of water.

Smaller eyes, just like Apachita's eyes, the same almonds with a dark brown centre, stare out of a window. They are looking for something. Their mother. Their father. Their teacher. The roof is so high above their head in the polytunnel as they crawl low to the floor, gulping the air, toward the mud fields. And to someone so small, climbing up the propagating ladders is like climbing a glacier all to reach one small sunburnt tomato. Seven years young, hand held out in a fist of victory, but they fall like a ragdoll, and the mud field is such a hard cake now, it does not break their fall so well.

Seven months wide the second time around. Terracotta peaty red blends in with the mud. Apachita's blood, if the floor were all white, would have spelled out a message, signalling, *Help*. And her mother's mother had carried the ice down with the men from the very top to ensure the fertility of their women and that of the land. Cast a spell. Had it broken.

Then the shedding stopped, and her layers stopped building. And the ground was too hot and dry. Apachita no longer made smalls and lost them. Yet still, she prayed to me. Water and life would be returned unto her on her sky cometh day. She was the one to touch the last dots of my white on the lower grounds in Winter when the Southern Hemisphere's last June had water which met with the cold.

The small, neat blonde woman says she is very interested

in genealogy. She is trying to find the key to her past. Her blonde hair is not natural. She is at pains to tell the guide that underneath, she is dark like the women who came before her, she is. Do you have any evidence? He asks.

Well, she has no roots. She takes her appearance very seriously; instead, she shows him a photo on a screen of her as a child. I stare at her intently like a lie detector. I remember all beings, humans and others, who have gone by here.

She does remind me a little of a pilgrim some centuries ago. Or perhaps a coloniser.

*Well, it does look a little like you*, he muses, *but we have to be so careful. If people can claim a connection to here, they will. We've had all kinds, and then you find out afterwards their kinfolk were from Old Florida. They'd try anything just to be accepted somewhere, even five degrees cooler.*

She is pushy. Pays for the platinum VIP experience. In the dried mud house, which has been preserved with top technological coating, she stands in the main room at the standing desk, and tears roll down her cheek. An alarmed glass surround case makes it so she can't reach out and touch the picture of Mariano. The data from the vintage Mac has been magnified, and on the walls, it is played in short, sharp bursts of stills like a silent horror film that can't be unwatched. In theory, she's already seen the film, but it's one of those movies where the human doesn't realise they've watched it already until a certain scene.

And then it all comes flooding back.

Has she had the test? The guide asks her. Like me, she was becoming undone. Desperate. They couldn't fix on the point her people had retreated from here, she told him. Just as they couldn't fix on the point I started to expire, the how, where, when, and why. They just had to take her word for it, she says. View absence as evidence. If her DNA didn't show certain markers, though, she'd be turned away.

Who were they to say who the land and its spirit belonged to? Back on the tourist boat home, to summer over there, on the other side. Since I had been gone, they didn't know which summer would be their last.

The blonde woman pricks her finger and prays.

The pilgrimage has become very competitive. People lie to get a spot. About who they were, who their people were. Their peoples role in what happened to me. One man had plastic surgery to try to get around certain identifiers commonly used. Though now exclusive, the festival carried on; people still searched for and celebrated the stars. And every June, a constellation the locals called *Qullqa* would appear, and the skies still darkened at night enough to see it.

The chosen few danced until the rising of the sun after the full moon. And called out *Qoyllur R'iti*, and remembered Mariano, whose body had been buried under the rock which I once lay atop. Heads all bowed, in a moment's silence—they look up to greet the first rays of light as the sun rises above the horizon.

And they must make their way forward in the heat in the full heavy costume of the elders as penance. Carrying back wooden crosses and blocks of ice, pretending they are not pre-frozen but simply lost and found, and they place them all along the road to the shrine. Flowers wilt on the plaque commemorating me. Dedicated to, *Dear future*.

# STILLS

*What did the lady say?*

*A secret. A secret prayer just for me,* said the girl.

*The Virgin Mary couldn't have spoken in local dialect because God and the Virgin don't speak local dialect,* interrupted the interrogator.

*How can we know and speak local dialect if they don't speak it?* replied the girl. *Do you think she spoke to me in French? Do I speak French?*

§

Once, a bright light pierced the darkness like a fire in the air. The villagers told this story with a dreamy look in their eyes. During the night, the breath of the miraculous blew over a sleepy market town in the foothills of the Hautes-Pyrénées. Some witnessed a glowing opposite the grotto, but it could have just been a freakish weather occurrence.

A woman appeared and spoke in their local Occitan dialect to a child who had requested that she make the rose bushes bloom again. Should there be a picture of the town now, it would show and hide a scorched early Christian church, a Roman road, an Immaculate Conception, a Pagan temple, and a fortified castle all against the backdrop of the picturesque Piémont Pyrénéen pilgrim route.

Various alpine greens, both lush and languishing, act as way-markers, competing with each other to climb limestone, granite, and gneiss-formed peaks, covering layer after layer of rock formations, like icing trying to race to the top of a gâteau à la broche. Layers of land are supple like dough and roasted one at a time by an open fire until finally, finally, gold crème adorns a spiky summit.

The vision had said, *I am the Immaculate Conception*, and then folded her wings back into herself softly and silently, and birdlike, flew away.

The Gave de Pau ran past, filled with freshness from its source at the Cirque de Gavarnie in the mountains. Its trickle back there had nourished the new lavender-blue hues of alpine snowbells as they acclimatised to more sunlight.

Pastures were high, and sheep were large in their flocks. 1844.

A candle fell in the mill and set a woman's life source ablaze. Her chest became a charred valley. Thick with smoke.

A fire lookout, positioned a thousand metres up high on the summit of Pic du Jur, was looking back in time and saw two twin charcoal-grey tendrils twisting delicately up, up in the air, rising from the vicinity of the small town of Lourdes. The woman pushed both her breasts far out, back arched, serenely, as though trying to escape her own flames and understanding the importance of calm in her situation.

There were singeing sounds over where she usually sang this time of night, a French lullaby: *sizzle—Meunier tu dors, hiss—Ton moulin va trop vite.*

*Spit.*

Her tune trailed off as the shock of the stinging singe subsided: *Miller, you're sleeping / Your mill spins too quickly,* and on the last C note, she brought the miller from his bed.

Milk ducts sighed wearily whilst waiting for the miller's water pail and let down little moon-white streams, self-extinguishing a last ember or two, and then set to work on healing the skin of her breasts.

The woman looked over at the swaddled saint, still sleeping, and reminded herself that at least she had given her the gold before this accident. But now, a new nurse would have to wet her baby. And the saint would not receive gold again until her still body was exhumed and housed in a glass coffin. Encased in gold. So far away from this prison of poverty, but locked, locked in aloneness.

The saint's mother is looking back down. At her tips, where crevices were already cracked and bleeding from overgrazing, and had melted and melded. Scar tissue was forming in the land of her heart. Striking a line through her bosom, then back over across the way it once lay, but adding a thick extra ridge. Purple. The colour faded over the years but still remained and reminded her.

In a notebook, the fire lookout scribbled down what they saw. Their views to the left, toward the past, snared both the towns of Bartrès and Lourdes. Then they glanced to the right and caught a glimpse of the future. Saw nothing but neon orange, like a complete blackout, but neon orange. A static image. And they decided it would be futile to raise any alarm.

As the saint always said, *I cannot lead them.*

The fire lookout glanced once more through the station binoculars, then scanned the horizon with a fire finder, azimuth *spinning*, looking right down the now dog-brown valley, noticing that the twin tendrils of smoke from before had put themselves out.

*Did you recite the beads in the fields of Bartrès? Yes, Monsieur,* said the girl.

178

Three male investigators take down notes of her different answers:

*I don't know.*
*She does not know.*
*She does not remember.*

The village doctor arrived at the farmhouse a minute after the not-moving. Though it probably wouldn't have made a difference. Thick jellylike blood was all over the white sheets along with cord and grey tissue, and all this human material seemed to be moving despite the obvious other stillness he witnessed laid out on the bed.

Or was it a trick of his imagination, or his eyes fuzzy from the glare of the lamplight thrust into his retina as he darted up the stairs to the mother's aid? The cord seemed pulsing one minute and not the next—some witchery.

The doctor tested the baby and searched for any vital signs. Rubbed him this way and that. Nothing. He was running cold already, as the heat of the mother ebbed away from him.

Perfect lips changed from rosebuds to river blue. A maid handed the doctor a shawl, and the mother stared wide-eyed into the distance, through the doorway towards her daughters, who would never be what a son could be.

She had dreamed about the boy since forever.

In her dreams, after the stilling, he was so healthy and strong. He tended to the sheep and cattle on the family farm. Helped his father collect the firewood. Knew all his prayers.

Protected his elder sisters and would not hear a bad word said against his mother or her housekeeping.

The baby's little fist was balled up, and the mother gently unravelled it like a complicated knitting ball and stroked each tiny fingernail in slow motion, so shiny, like miniature pearls. In the space on the sheets where he had been pushed out lifeless, remained an imprint of his limbs, of his body, of his head—a shape of him preserved by the stain of his mother.

Now he only exists in her dreams. And from then on, she dedicated her nights to visions of him, long, lonely dreams, which she only partially woke from each morning, deep diving back in to delay the pain of waking without hearing his cry.

After they took the body away, she filled up and up. She was so heavy.

The mother looked about her for a pin in desperation, for anything, and imagined herself popping each swollen breast like making a balloon go bang on Bastille Day and letting all the air go out of it at once.

The relief. The forced celebration.

Looking down at this other thing, both a consolation and a thorn at her breast. Five francs a week to nurse a saint. The longer she wet her tiny mouth, the longer the pain lasted; the longer she suckled, the longer the pain lasted.

And one day, she vowed she would bring the child back to make her pay her dues in other ways.

The child grew.

*Would you like to tend sheep with me?*

They were in an intermediate state between life and death: the ewe and its lamb. Just the one lamb this time around. She had been a good mother before. The ewe tried to lick the lamb's nose after, even so. It did not lift its head nor bleat for its mother. And could not be revived through drying and warming with a shawl. A cold, bitter wind blew in from the North, and the Hautes-Pyrénées put up their shoulders like a crowd trying to give privacy to a man knocked down by a cart on market day.

The lamb left a stamp in the late snow as the shepherdess saint gently shifted its body from side to side. Just to check, to be sure. Left a crimson red imprint of its little legs in the frost and would remind the ewe, until it was cleaned away by the rain or by tread and wear, what her baby would have been shaped like. The girl imagined the little lamb rising, standing, and attached to its mother, tasting milk from the teat. The pulling and tickling sensations the ewe might have felt.

The ewe's head was hanging down now, and she let out a mournful bleat and moved with great pain over to the space on the ground where the body had lain and sniffed and then kicked her hind hoof in anger.

The ewe had so much gold to give.

The girl placed her shawl over the body, never minding the mess and fluids, and caressed the ewe with a gentle stroke across her face and a kiss, and then said the rosary with a hand on her second bead.

*Hail Mary, full of grace, the Lord is with Thee. Blessed art Thou among women, and blessed is the fruit of Thy womb, Jesus. Holy Mary, Mother of God, pray for us sinners now and at the hour of our death. Amen.*

The girl, this shepherdess saint, heard that down the road in Tarbes, a farmer was searching for a wet nurse for an orphan lamb, its mother having been lost; that ewe had closed her eyes during the last night, eternally tired. The orphan lamb had been pulled hard at the moment the mother's breath was leaving her, and they had held eye contact for a second as the orphan was lifted out and over her body as though levitating.

That ewe was so sleepy, dreaming almost lucidly, she stirred and saw her lamb alive and kicking outside of her, stretching and expanding its small lungs with her breath, methodically drawing her last breath inside it until she had none left for herself. And in that moment, that ewe thought her lamb was a vision of beauty. In that ewe's dream, she tried to redirect the lamb to back inside of her womb, where they were both safe, but then she fell asleep forever.

At the farm of the shepherdess saint, a little later on that year, they needed to move the cattle shed and so exhumed the bodies of the animals buried there. A dirty job. Flies. Maggots. But one lost lamb, dug up, remained pure. The shawl it was wrapped in had started to disintegrate, but the body lay bare and incorrupt, with its cloppers all perfect still, and its face looking up all smooth and clean as though it had just been born and licked fresh by its mother.

*Would you like to see the conversion of sinners?*
*Yes, Monsieur,* said the girl.

In the town of Nevers, a shepherdess is dug up with the mayor as a key witness. The mouth was open slightly, and it could be seen that the teeth were still in place. A gap in her mouth made space to utter her last words.

*Penance, Penance, Penance, all this is good for Heaven! Blessed Mary, Mother of God, Pray for me,* the girl said.

According to witnesses – the mayor, his deputy, and several canons – the habit was damp. Only the face, hands, and forearms were uncovered. The head tilted to the left—the face dull white. The skin clinging to the muscles, and the muscles adhering to the bones. The eye sockets were covered by the eyelids as though resting in peaceful sleep. The brows were flat on the skin and stuck to the arches above the eyes as if given to rise at any moment in question or mirth. The lashes of the right eyelid were attached to the skin as though frozen with tears. The nose was dilated and shrunken. The hands, which were crossed over her breast, were perfectly preserved, as were the nails. The hands still held a rusting rosary. *Tightly.* The veins on the forearms stood out as though still pumping with blood.

She smiled in her sleep as though dreaming of digging the ground herself as a child with her bare hands and turning dry soil into a wet spring gifted from her lady, and carrying up from the ground and cradling in her arms a *still*, perfect lamb.

# The ancestor's apparition

She is just standing there, on the edge of the train platform in a French town called Nevers. It's the first time the girl has seen her since. Except her kaftan top isn't her kaftan top. And her faded green Doc Martens are not the ones on the woman's feet. The face is still a star-freckled, elegant oval held up by a defiant tilt of chin. The girl's puzzled as she contemplates this mirage. Trying to figure it out. Hair. Exactly the same. A cross between Ann Robinson and lesbian chic. Red. Cropped short. But she's too quiet.

The girl has come to see a saint about a sign, and she's just been through it all, and she's on her way home now. Just said goodbye to Bernadette in her crystal casket. Told her she'd be back and not to worry, try not to feel too lonely, I know it's hard. Anyway, this woman, she's standing there in the very last moment of the girl's self-proclaimed pilgrimage, and she looks just like her mum, but her mum is dead. And in all these years, she's never seen anyone who looked anything close to her.

She looks down at the woman's legs suspiciously. At the bottom of her feet are two blue suede sensible house-wife-type shoes. And she wears some sort of slacks. She looks very French. The girl can't know she is French because this woman makes no noise. She is the most silent thing in the train station. You wouldn't mess with her, though; she holds herself in a way that says so. They have that in common, but she's so still.

Not like the girl's mum. She'd be feeding the station people out of her hand by now. Like the pigeon lady in Mary Poppins, feed the birds, charm the people.

Dead Bernadette has more life than this apparition. Station pigeons skirt around the woman and pretend not to see the breadcrumbs close to her blue suede shoes. The air around her is an invisible casket, and it makes her limbs lean in and stop rigid like a corpse in rigor mortis. But then, all of a sudden, a rigor arm moves forward ever so slowly; it holds out a phone.

The girl remembers the time she picked up her ex's mobile because they'd had the same model, and on the screen, it had said, *Mum calling*. And she thought it was her, and she was scared and full of fucking hope until the very last ring. Then she was just standing there afterwards, just standing there. She'd dropped the phone back onto the work surface like a burning brick.

The girl has that same look on her face just now.

The woman's mouth opens, but no sound emits; a disembodied voice announces the next train pulling into the platform, to Paris. The rigor limb is typing on the phone now. The eyes. Aesthetically, they look the same, the same off-green with a hint of grey, but they don't laugh; they are dead, and now the girl's convinced the apparition isn't an apparition after all. It's a robot simulation of her mum placed here by some evil force as if to say, *If you look for signs, then this is what you will get.*

*It's a cruel trick,* she tells herself. This is all some sort of cruel trick.

There are mini madeleines in the platform vending machine. Proust is peddling the past. She inserts €1.20.

She shouldn't have looked. She shouldn't have looked.


*Pure in blood, pure in blood,* the soul of Cacciaguida tells Dante. He is interviewing the apparition of his great-great-grandfather for Paradiso no. 16. And then the moustachioed artist takes the apparition of Dante's ancestor and turns it into a woodcut engraving, a splash of almost fluorescent yellow to highlight the miraculousness of it all, arms up at the vision.

And then the girl walks into a gallery dedicated to the moustachioed artist in Bruges, having never brought art before, well, art, art anyway. It feels good, and there is a jolt of something that pulses through and out of her body as she hands over her card for four figures.

The letter comes in the post, from the catalogue of the moustachioed artist, to confirm her ownership of his art piece. And she reads it back to herself, *I am the owner of The Ancestor's Apparition by the moustachioed artist, and I have the piece of paper to prove it.* Heaven, Hell, and Purgatory. These are the themes of his one hundred watercolours in response to Dante Alighieri's Divine Comedy. But, when she first browses the wood engravings, she doesn't think about those things. Just uses her intuition. Walks up and down. Looking but not looking, just waiting to be drawn to something.

*This one, please.*

And she takes it home on the mini cruise ferry from Bruges to Hull, then in the car with her other ex, and he is tense because she got an art piece; he got one too after she paid, a bit more expensive, he saw how she was metamorphosing, how the saleswoman had to pull the girl's chair out further than her body required from the table, in order to accommodate all the energy, so she could get the girl to sign the papers for the art, and the girl signed with a flourish.

As they left, brown papered cylinders in arms, the saleswoman and the girl exchanged knowing glances at his slightly bigger-than-hers package.

Sometimes bigger isn't always better.

When she gets home, the girl puts the art piece in a drawer with its certificate, along with the book on the Divine Comedy she got to better understand the inspiration behind the piece she ended up with. And they all sit there for years, unlooked at, unread. Until she forgets their names, and forgets their images, and forgets herself. Then one day, she decides to look. There is water damage due to the neglect in how it has been kept. And she wonders if the moustachioed artist would be disappointed in her or perhaps even impressed. And then, she sees a message: an apparition in the art piece title- She unconsciously chose an art piece of an apparition without realising it was about an apparition: 'The Ancestors Apparition' (1963). And this girl, Bernadette, she shares her name with perhaps the most famous of all those who have witnessed apparitions.

Saint Bernadette.

This sign could only mean one thing: she must seek further signs.

She is inching herself towards the big platform, the one that takes you to the Big City, and it stands on its own, as if to say its end destination is far more superior than the Northern towns, other places, the ones you can reach by leaving from platforms one to seven.

The girl studies the people on the platform waiting to board the train to London Euston and wonders what business they have going there. Trains that way are not cheap. Perhaps they are a corporate hero, and once onboard, she will hear them talking in that dot the I's and cross the T's lingo. Or maybe, they like shopping in Harrods, or they feel as though they should, and they will step on the train hair all coiffed and lips all bigged and post pictures on the gram. And they will come home with bags that speak.

And then there is her.

She looks at a photo of a large, sprawling convent on her phone, along with a body in a glass coffin, and takes a sip of her oat latte.

The girl's business is different.


London St Pancras. There is a stampede. Of coronavirus particles as the next herd of Eurostar passengers moves into the train boarding waiting area. She can tell the French apart from the British by 3M masks or paper masks, and style.

The girl is seated with three French people who must be business colleagues. She is meant to be sitting in the window seat, but the only woman with them takes it. She wants to look out of the window to see what's outside, wants to note it down, to take observations of the travelling environment as she goes. But their reflections block her line of sight, and it is like she is them, them looking in a mirror, and she feels as though she has intruded on an intimate moment. The girl averts her eyes and leaves them to their unconscious introspection.

Until the sun starts to go down and the light through the window takes away their shadows, and then the view is all of theirs.

The sunset casts amber jewels, which makes the rising floodwaters on Botany Marshes out past Gravesend dapple, and the girl notes that they are high for this time of spring. As the Eurostar snakes through the last low grasses of Southern England, the waters keep on rising.

They are risen.

Paris Gare du Nord.

The girl decides to walk to the hotel. It's getting dark, but the streets are brightly lit and busy. The walk is less than eighteen minutes, and the metro would take twenty. And she can see and breathe, the scent of today's pâtisseries closing, all that Paris air in.

A black leather-jacketed man is waiting outside the station, and the girl doesn't manage to slip by. The streets become a maze, the walk becomes a chase, and she breaks into a canter. She cuts through one side street, and then he cuts through the opposite side and comes out the other side, and meets her in the middle.

He grins. Cat and mouse.

She veers off to a left side street quickly, as if she was going to walk right on; he takes another twist.

He knows this labyrinth too well.

The girl crosses the main boulevard and looks up into the CCTV cameras to show the look in her eyes, *He is winning*, her eyes say, but no one reads them. Someone must be watching.

Don't they see more than her? Than the object moving? Don't they see why the object moves? Boulevards, criss-crossing, side streets, side-stepping, and on and on, until her travel bag makes her shoulder bleed, and it takes forty minutes instead of eighteen, but she loses him.

And she's so tired when she arrives at the top of the hotel, and dripping with adrenaline, but she's at the top, the top floor, and she pushes the door and double windows open. And the church bells of Saint-Jean de Montmartre chime and strike eight, and she has reached the castle and defeated the Goblin King, and so she says it out loud, *You have no power over me. You have no power over me.*

The Eiffel Tower is in her eyeline, all lit up, ready for some more objectification. *Look at my pretty, long iron legs,* it says coyly, *but don't look, look.* A light strobe comes from the upper levels of the tower, plays the people at their own game, and scans the streets from the top like a police helicopter searching.

She settles. The tower and the girl are in this together. A soft breeze cools her face, and a large plane tree just outside the window shakes its pom-poms at her and offers calm and counsel.

The next day, she wakes up, and the sun is shining, and she feels happy. The girl walks around Montmartre, drinking coffee in the gardens, and walks up the hill, and a street artist stops her. The girl walked by him three times already today, but something about him now makes her stop, and before she knows it, the word, *Yes*, has escaped from her lips. Other people look on, *Yes*, this is some spectacle: a tourist has been successfully trapped.

She is made to stand in the street very still and look at a house number painted on a wall, number thirteen, and she thinks this must be a sign because she's lived in a couple of houses with the number thirteen, and she never lasted very long there. A small crowd gathers. They look over the shoulder of the artist, whose name she will see signed there after, right by her face, Michael. And then Michael becomes the watched as he sketches in the crowd. The watchers watch the watcher. And he watches the girl intently, traces the outline of her face with a pencil, and then starts to move his hand more rapidly as he shades in the girl's cheekbones and roughs out her smile. Because she's smiling, she's smiling in the street. And the people watching the watcher while she is watched, they all smile too.

The girl gives Michael double and takes the picture. He asks her name, *Bernadette*. She replies, *Bernadette*.

The girl is all rolled up in her own handbag, with an elastic band securing her face, and it causes the paper to tear a little, and her hair is ripped, but she doesn't care, it still means as much to her. Maybe she'll frame it, or perhaps she'll keep herself in a little drawer next to the apparition, and if people ever need to resummon her once she's gone, they can take her out and press out the creases in the paper and just look at her.

And then she dances up the hill to the moustachioed artist's museum.

She's at the reception, and there is no queue. It is so hot and sunny no one wants to be inside; this is the first summer of spring this year. The receptionist says to the girl, *You don't need the mask in here.*

The girl pays, and she enters.

She is following the rooms around, and then the girl is lost and found by an engraving, and she stands with them until her own self collects her. The engraving is entitled, *The Girl on the Rhino Casanova.* And there's a naked woman up there, straddling a rhino with her legs open and stretched wide, and she is so full of that rhino. So exposed to the rhino and exposed to the watchers. But her face is disconnected from her body, and she looks as though she might fall off his tail, which is coming away at the tip.

And the girl is reading; she's reading about how the moustachioed artist made this artwork based on stories written by another man, who once said, *Cultivating whatever gave pleasure to my senses was always the chief business of my life.*

Nevers. The gates to the convent.

The convent wall has an arched, open doorway in its stones, reminding the girl of the steps leading up to the carved-in entry to St. Nick's Church, the sailors' church in Liverpool. But there is no sea here or the Mersey, just a small winding regular road filled with everyday townspeople going about their daily business.

But they look.

She is a girl they do not recognise, and visitors are rarer this time of year outside of the religious festival season. They are not looking, looking. Just looking and observing, and passing by, taking quiet note.

Check-in. She is given a map of the footsteps Bernadette walked in and is invited to follow her steps around the convent grounds and follow her and follow her and follow her until, at last, she would find her sleeping on the last point of the map. And then she may do as she wishes.

The lady at the reception does not ask about the girl's intentions. Just tells her the breakfast times and gives her a key and directions to her room.

And the girl asks about seeing Bernadette. Outside of the treasure map game, because she is here for a few days, and seeing her at the end of the map game feels too orchestrated, and she's not sure they'd be able to have the conversation she wants to have. *You are a guest,* the reception lady tells her. *The chapel is open to you at all times.* She can visit Bernadette at 1:00 a.m., 8:00 p.m., 4:21 a.m., 5:30 p.m., 3:00 a.m., or at any time she wishes.

The girl can just go to her.

She absorbs this information and heads down a long, long parquet corridor to find her room. The girl is tired after the train from Liverpool to London, then from London to Paris, and then from Paris to Nevers. And the cat and mouse game. And the being drawn, playing the object, all the standing, all the staring at the number thirteen on the wall, and the being watched and pretending not to watch back.

She hears a click-clack of heels from behind, and it's the lady from reception, *Bernadette, Bernadette!* She calls. She means her. She catches up to the girl, breathless. She holds something out in her hand. And she says, *I forgot, I forgot to tell you, a pen, everyone with the name Bernadette who stays here, they get a free pen.*

The girl looks at the pen. It has a wood effect covering, and the words, *Bernadette,* are stencilled along its length, top-sided with the logo of Bernadette's dead, unmoving body.

She thanks her, and she takes the pen. The girl is playing with time.

Trying to save the moment she's been thinking about. She doesn't want this to be it.

The girl decides to visit the grounds museum and gift shop first. Bernadette's incorrupt body is available in all sizes and styles in the gift shop. Fridge magnet. A3 poster, laminated. Embroidered onto rosary beads, two for one. There are postcards with several variations of her image and sayings, books with different quotes in from Bernadette, typed below her laid-back-in-rest head: the quotes say things like, *They think I'm a saint… When I'm dead, they'll come and touch holy pictures and rosaries to me, and all the while, I'll be getting broiled on a grill in purgatory.*

Well, Saint Bernadette said that in real life, it was recorded, but no, that isn't one of the quotes they use to project her body and its suffering. It's things like, *Why do we have to suffer? Because down here, pure Love does not exist without suffering.* Or another classic on a tea towel, *It is so good, so sweet and above all, so beneficial to suffer.*

The girl picks up several postcards and bookmarks. She can't face a large poster right now. It feels too contrived or like something she'd order secretly on the internet and frame in her home if she ever got around to it. Or she could lock Bernadette's image in the drawer in a cardboard cylinder as she did with the moustachioed artist and just suck the energy out when she really needed it, when she was about to break. Bernadette shouldn't mind. After all, she's a saint, isn't she?

Anyhow, the girl just gets all the small things, duplicate images of Bernadette, hands clasped together in different-sized cards, with her wax face overlay central to the pictures, remodelled by a French fashion designer after the nuns touched her too much, corroded her too much.

And it's this newer face on the cards, but it's like Bernadette's first face because they remade it, and the girl wonders what it feels like to lie down and have a version of your own face resting on your face.

What it would be like, to peel that layer back and expose your own disintegrating face, to yourself, to the world.

The girl has played the role of consumer of the saint. She thanks the ladies in the shop and takes her receipt. Clutches her plastic bag closed over, should any other visitor see the purchases inside, perhaps ones with more dignity, more self-control. But the girl had become complicit in the consumption of Bernadette's unburying, of keeping her exposed, objectified.

Because buried underneath, with the worms and the other bodies, the ones that decayed, there would be no postcards, nothing to sell.

No sign to show good pilgrims that if you are virtuous and accept your suffering, you will be immortalised forever.

The girl imagines handing the little postcards with Bernadette's face on to her friends and family once home. Like she'd just come back from the Balearics.

She decides to brave the map. And she's walking and walking. She's walking in Bernadette's footsteps. It's hot in the grounds, so hot for this time of spring, and no one else is here but the girl. Just her and Bernadette. Well, she hasn't gone to her yet. She's just skirting around that bit, just hanging out in the gardens, following the points on the set guided map in order, as any good visitor would. And she's trying to imagine what it would've been like living here with the other nuns for Bernadette. In hiding from the mass mobs at Lourdes, all after a slice of her healing powers, of her capacity to show a willingness to suffer.

And the girl doesn't think Bernadette was like the other nuns. Some of the *Bernadette's Sayings* books in the gift shop show some resistance. The girl thinks bad things about her, as in she doesn't think Bernadette was always good. Perhaps Bernadette held secrets, behind the convent walls.

Perhaps she felt an unwavering love for another other than her beloved God. And maybe, when the lights went out, Bernadette relieved her own suffering before the morning prayers started. The apparition had said to Saint Bernadette, *I cannot promise to make you happy in this world, only in the next, now you will pray to God for sinners.* And so, she did, and maybe, maybe, she made herself happy in this world, in the darkness, when the nights were long, and breathing did not come so easily.

The girl turns a corner and comes to a replica grotto of Lourdes. There is a white marble statue of Bernadette kneeling in prayer and surrounded by sacrificial offerings from pilgrims: candles, letters, and notes of prayer. And the girl pauses. She has taken the paths that were expected of her.

She doesn't feel like the time is quite right, though. And not because of questioning Bernadette's character, or rather the memorialisation of her character.

The girl just doesn't feel ready. She needs coffee.

She searches and passes an exhibit of the snuff box Bernadette used to store the snuff she took as an aid to help her asthma, she walks past a large blown-up poster of her, uncharacteristically of from when she was alive, and in a small dark corner of the Bernadette museum, the girl finds an eighties-style coffee machine.

She inserts €1.20.

She shouldn't have thought. She shouldn't have thought.


It is time.

The corridor leading to the interior chapel is so long and narrow, and it seems to go on forever. It reminds her of the corridor leading to her mum's hospital ward, so long it needed a bridge to carry it, and the girl always imagined the hospital planners with their design plan saying, *This will give them enough time to steady themselves.*


She is at her final approach.

An ethereal light shines through a gap in the slightly ajar door, and it is like in films when the bright white light calls to a person in their last moments. And the girl walks towards it. She is ready.

She sees her.

Walks around the chapel first, taking note of its environment, before getting closer. The girl feels like Goldilocks entering the bears' cottage. There are many places to sit: a soft, circular, red fabric stool, a row of hard, dark wooden pews, and some ornately designed, high-backed chairs. And she tries each one in turn, soft circular, too soft, dark pew, too hard, high back, too rigid, and then the floor by Bernadette's coffin, just right.

The girl gets it wrong at first and does what she thinks is the right thing to do when in the presence of a saint in a chapel. She kneels and says the Lord's Prayer before her. She looks up slyly, under her lashes, in between verses, no reaction. Bernadette knows she is acting.

The girl gets up and walks around, taking photos of the smaller details on her phone. The priest's cloak hung up, a notebook lying on the side with ideas for a new sermon. No one else is home right now after hours. And it's just her, just her and Bernadette.

There are still no signs.

She wasn't real with Bernadette. She just did what the pope wanted all along. The girl looks closely at the glass coffin. Bernadette's screwed in.

She thinks.

The girl gets up.

She starts to say goodbye, just casually, she's talking to Bernadette like a normal person, *Well, I'll be back tomorrow, hope you get a good night's sleep.* Then the girl notices something, Bernadette's chest. It seems to move in tiny, microscopic breaths, and it makes her move closer to check, past the do not move past this line sign. And she's staring at Bernadette's chest because she knows she must be imagining it. The girl knows that.

It's just a trick, just a trick of the mind, but it all started when the girl started talking to her, just like she was anybody else.

Then Bernadette's face, underneath the wax overlay, which was firm in its expression before, it starts to change ever so softly, like a person at the end of life, on the morphine driver, and they're falling, falling, into a deep, dreamy sleep. But in their ear, they hear the voice of a loved one. And their expression, it changes ever so slightly, almost imperceptible, to show they can sense something, someone, and it's all they can manage. And Bernadette's face is just like that.

Just like that.

And the girl says to her, *Goodbye Bernadette, I'll see you, I'll see you tomorrow.*

On the last day, the pews are up against the chapel side door blocking the entrance, and the girl has to climb over. Two ladies are cleaning about Bernadette, one hoovers with a long extension lead, and another uses a feather duster to sweep the red brick eaves. And the girl doesn't want to leave her like this. She's so lonely, Bernadette seems so lonely.

It is like when she left her mother in the hospital morgue all alone, and she had felt so guilty.

The girl is in the street in Paris after getting the train back from Nevers, and everything is so heavy and hot, and her bag is hurting her shoulder again, and she's carrying too many things. Saints' sufferings and artist sketches, and her big winter scarf, it is burning a hole in her neck.

And it is strangling her under all that weight. So she unravels it and stuffs it, inch by inch, into an almost full bin until it's all coiled up like some long, abandoned snake.

And the girl walks away as people watch the woman who could no longer bear her own scarf.

Paris Charles de Gaulle Airport.

The girl is lying on the hotel bed, watching the sunset over the runway, with a facemask on. She is preparing to be viewed.

She will become his object.

When she lands in that other place.

And she's tired. And her face, it looks so swollen.

From the pollen, from Parc de Bercy, which made her cry, on the way here. The girl spotted the facemask on the minimarket shelf and was called to it. The instructions said, *Adjust the mask to the contours of your own face.*

*Press the cooling eye sockets to your own eyes—wet paper bone to bone. Smooth its edges around your hairline and tuck it under your chin.*

*Fit it to fit yourself.*

And then afterwards, the mask maker tells the girl, *she will be renewed, revitalised, her cells regenerated.*

So, the girl lies there with the facemask on, and she thinks of Saint Bernadette. The girl is worried about her, her loneliness, and about how she has left her behind.

And she knows now how heavy a mask feels when on.

And how it makes you want to take a peek at the time, because ten minutes feels too long, but everyone knows, if you take it off too early, you could ruin things for yourself, and you'll lose maybe one, maybe two minutes of its impact.

Of its goodness.


The girl half stands up and looks in the mirror, sort of tilting her chin up as she edges off the bed so as not to knock the mask off before it's time.

She wants to rip that overlay face right off her own face. But the time isn't up yet.

Instead, she starts peeling ever so delicately. The girl begins tugging it, away from her face, in tiny, tiny fractions.

Until she's back.

Then she's peeling, peeling, peeling again, until Bernadette's free. And then the girl says, *You're free.*

BERNADETTE MCBRIDE is an award-winning writer, filmmaker, academic, and creative practitioner based in the UK. She won the Biggest Impact on the City of Liverpool Award in 2019 for her creative writing programmes in the community. She was shortlisted for the prestigious Manchester Fiction Prize in 2020 for her story, 'For the man who died in the wood.' Her short fiction has appeared in anthologies and journals. Her story, 'Sea monster,' was adapted for film and selected for several international film festivals. This is her first full short story collection.

www.bernadettemcbride.co.uk